PRAISE F
STREE1
A(

MW00465374

Seabreeze Inn and *Coral Cottage* **series**

"A wonderful story… Will make you feel like the sea breeze is streaming through your hair." – Laura Bradbury, Bestselling Author

"A novel that gives fans of romantic sagas a compelling voice to follow." – *Booklist*

"An entertaining beach read with multi-generational context and humor." – *InD'Tale* Magazine

"Wonderful characters and a sweet story." – Kellie Coates Gilbert, Bestselling Author

"A fun read that grabs you at the start." – Tina Sloan, Author and Award-Winning Actress

"Jan Moran is the queen of the epic romance." —Rebecca Forster, *USA Today* Bestselling Author

"The women are intelligent and strong. At the core is a strong, close-knit family." — Betty's Reviews

The Chocolatier

"A delicious novel, makes you long for chocolate." – *Ciao Tutti*

"Smoothly written…full of intrigue, love, secrets, and romance." – *Lekker Lezen*

The Winemakers

"Readers will devour this page-turner as the mystery and passions spin out." – *Library Journal*

"As she did in *Scent of Triumph*, Moran weaves knowledge of wine and winemaking into this intense family drama." – *Booklist*

The Perfumer: Scent of Triumph

"Heartbreaking, evocative, and inspiring, this book is a powerful journey." – Allison Pataki, *NYT* Bestselling Author of *The Accidental Empress*

"A sweeping saga of one woman's journey through World War II and her unwillingness to give up even when faced with the toughest challenges." — Anita Abriel, Author of *The Light After the War*

"A captivating tale of love, determination and reinvention." — Karen Marin, Givenchy Paris

"A stylish, compelling story of a family. What sets this apart is the backdrop of perfumery that suffuses the story with the delicious aromas – a remarkable feat!" — Liz Trenow, *NYT* Bestselling Author of *The Forgotten Seamstress*

"Courageous heroine, star-crossed lovers, splendid sense of time and place capturing the unease and turmoil of the 1940s; HEA." — *Heroes and Heartbreakers*

BOOKS BY JAN MORAN

Crown Island Series

Beach View Lane

Sunshine Avenue

Orange Blossom Way

Summer Beach Series

Seabreeze Inn

Seabreeze Summer

Seabreeze Sunset

Seabreeze Christmas

Seabreeze Wedding

Seabreeze Book Club

Seabreeze Shores

Seabreeze Reunion

Seabreeze Honeymoon

Seabreeze Gala

Coral Cottage Series

Coral Cottage

Coral Cafe

Coral Holiday

JAN MORAN

SUNSHINE
Avenue

SUNSHINE AVENUE

CROWN ISLAND SERIES
BOOK 2

JAN MORAN

SUNNY PALMS

PRESS

Library of Congress Cataloging-in-Publication Data
Moran, Jan.
/ by Jan Moran

ISBN 978-1-64778-122-4 (epub ebook)
ISBN 978-1-64778-124-8 (hardcover)
ISBN 978-1-64778-123-1 (paperback)
ISBN 978-1-64778-126-2 (audiobook)
ISBN 978-1-64778-125-5 (large print)

Published by Sunny Palms Press. Cover design by Okay Creations. Cover
images copyright Deposit Photos.

Sunny Palms Press
9663 Santa Monica Blvd STE 1158
Beverly Hills, CA 90210 USA
www.sunnypalmspress.com
www.JanMoran.com

1

"That's the house?" Junie's heart sank as she eased her grandmother's golf cart to the curb in front of a ramshackle cottage. Sun-bleached paint peeled from the wooden porch. She turned to her friend Jo, who owned Cuppa Jo's, a local diner on Crown Island. "It looks pretty rough."

"I told you it needs new paint," Jo replied. "It's fairly original. That's my house over there. The lavender one with yellow shutters. This one could look like that, too."

Other cottages on the street were splashed with sherbet colors of the rainbow, a Crown Island tradition. Junie wondered what color she might paint the old house. As she slid from the golf cart she used to run around the small island, her gaze fell on overgrown grass, tangled vines, and weed-infested gardens. As bad as it was, the empty lot next door was even worse.

"I'd have to hack my way through this jungle." Junie brushed tiny flying insects from her bare arms as she started up the broken pathway. "Think I could get the neighbors to clean up their place, too?"

"That's the best part of this deal." Jo gestured to the adjoining empty lot. "The land from here to that other house is included with this house. That house on the other side is for sale, too."

Junie glanced at the neat home that abutted the overgrown lot. The beautiful structure had wrap-around porches, a small but well-tended garden, and swings that hung from an old tree. Splashed in ocean blue with white and navy trim, the larger home could have been featured in a magazine. Even the For Sale sign was fancy.

"I'm sure that's much more than I want to spend," Junie said. She liked this smaller cottage. "That house is too large for just me."

Having not lived alone for years, Junie thought the larger home was a bit intimidating. For now, she was better suited toward the cozy little nest. She tried to picture it with a fresh coat of paint.

Peering beyond thickets that obscured her view of the adjoining land, she asked, "Is there anything back there?"

"Citrus trees line the rear." Jo kicked a fallen branch to one side of the walk. "Old Mrs. Ashbury's orchard produced the sweetest tangerines and orange, as well as lemon, lime, and grapefruit. She used to give me sacks of fruit, but after she died, the new tenants stopped tending to the trees. It was a real fairy tale of a garden, though. I'm sure you could bring it back."

The idea of picking fresh grapefruit for breakfast appealed to Junie. "I like working outside, even though I have a lot to learn."

A frisson of excitement coursed through her as she took

in the tired cottage. Sure, it needed work, but the size and location were ideal for her. The sound of the nearby ocean would be a pleasant lullaby. Plus, it would be a short bike ride to her grandmother Ella's home, where her mother and sister Maileah were staying. Although she loved her family, with Maileah's arrival from Seattle, the house was proving far too small for all of them.

Her sister couldn't afford to move because she'd lost her job, and their mother had committed to staying with Ella. If Junie wanted more room, she'd have to move.

She just wasn't sure if she was ready yet, even though living with Maileah and her moping around was difficult. Junie hadn't forgotten that her sister had initially sided with their philandering father in their parent's divorce.

"Watch your step," Jo said as she approached the porch with her light, energetic gait. Her short, dark hair gleamed in the sunshine.

The scent of thick green vegetation rose around them, and bees flitted among scraggly lavender bushes.

Junie stepped gingerly onto the front porch, taking care to avoid unstable planks and the rickety railing. Still, the cottage had potential.

While she didn't need the adjoining lot, she began to imagine how she might turn it into a magical garden. Bucolic images of fruit-laden trees and a rippling pond filled her mind. She could probably manage. Watch a few videos and buy some gardening books. How hard could it be?

Jo fished in her jeans pocket and produced a key. "I'll see if this still works. Mrs. Ashbury liked me to check on the house when she was away visiting her children. They're the heirs to her estate."

"Will they mind if we go in?"

"I called and asked," Jo replied. "Her son told me they might clean before listing it for sale, but he and his siblings don't want to make any repairs. They plan to sell it as it is. Because of that, I think you could get it for a great price."

Jo turned the key, and the door swung open.

Immediately, a stench wafted from the darkened interior, and the two women backed up. Junie pulled her thin cotton scarf from her long hair and pressed it over her nose. "Did something die in there?"

"I hope not," Jo said, suddenly looking doubtful. "The former tenants kept to themselves. I haven't been inside since Mrs. Ashbury passed away. The place was always neat and tidy when she lived here. Let's open some windows."

The wooden floor creaked under their footsteps. Junie pushed aside smoke-laden drapes and flung open a window. A shaft of sunlight fell on a mountain of garbage bags. Flies feasted on rotting food scraps in partially open bags.

"That's the problem," Junie said, holding her scarf to her nose again. "Looks like they had an aversion to taking out the garbage. Who lives like that?"

"People who don't want to pay for trash pickup." Jo shook her head. "They were a bunch of kids. There were a lot of them drifting in and out. I'll tell the family so they can have someone clean this up. That's the least they can do."

In the kitchen, a doggie door hung open to the outside. "That smell is probably attracting other critters, too," Junie said, shuddering at the thought of rats and raccoons traipsing through the house at night. "Let's make this quick."

They hurried through the house. Holding her breath,

Junie quickly counted a nice primary bedroom and two smaller ones, two bathrooms, and living and dining rooms. Most opened onto more overgrown gardens. Everything was dated but mostly serviceable. She made a mental list of what she would need: a refrigerator, washer, and dryer. And buckets of bleach and paint.

Junie burst through the front door and exhaled, then gulped in fresh ocean air. "That needs to be fumigated."

"But it could be charming," Jo said. "My place wasn't much better when I bought it." When Junie raised her brow, Jo added, "Though it didn't stink. Still, the heirs will take about half of what it would be worth if it were fixed up. I call that a stinkin' good deal."

Junie laughed at that. "Maybe that stench has some merit then." She glanced back at the house. Given a good cleaning, paint, and gardening, it could be adorable. And the location was perfect.

What would Mark have thought of this?

It had been more than two years since he'd died, yet she often wondered what he would think or advise her to do. They'd confided everything to each other. They'd had a real partnership and love-filled marriage, and she still missed him every day.

"I suppose I could work on it, but…" Junie paused and wagged her head.

Could she really do this without Mark, or was she deluding herself? She barely knew the difference between a regular screwdriver and those with four points, whatever they were called.

This wasn't what her therapist would call a baby step. This was a giant leap into what could be an endless money pit.

Junie could feel Jo's gaze on her. Maybe her friend sensed she had other concerns. Was that a trace of pity in her eyes? Junie hated that, as if being a widow somehow made her a victim of circumstance. Even if, technically, she was. But that made people treat her differently, and she was tired of it.

"I'd help you," Jo said. "Sailor and Blue and their buddies would probably pitch in, too."

"I don't know about that..."

Jo touched her shoulder with an empathetic gesture. "It's how we do things on the island. Ask your grandmother. Blue and some of the other guys on the police force have helped paint her house and do minor repairs."

"We're all grateful for that." Junie knew that Ella sometimes watched children or baked extra bread or cookies for people, especially Officer Blumenthal, or Blue, as he was known, and Sailor, a surfer who ran the bike concession at the Majestic Hotel. Sailor and Blue were among Ella's favorites.

A knot formed in Junie's chest as she thought about the empty house. Would people visit her here?

"This is such a great deal." Jo peered at her. "What's really holding you back?"

"I've never lived alone," Jo blurted out, fully aware of how infantile that sounded. She felt her face warm with embarrassment.

Jo arched an eyebrow. "How old are you again?"

"Thirty-two. But I went from my parents' home to having college roommates, and then I married. After Mark's accident, I moved home right away."

The quietness of the condominium she'd shared with her husband was more than she could bear. Sleeping alone was hard enough, but waking to the silent void only deepened her grief.

Junie recalled that with one look at her sunken eyes, her mother had insisted she return home to her old room where she could look after her.

Even then, Junie could hardly bring herself to change out of Mark's old shirts that she wore day after day. Now, she barely remembered that dark period, but the horror of the solitude she experienced was still fresh in her mind, as was her waning desire to live without him.

Fortunately, her mother had intervened and brought her to Crown Island to look after Ella, who'd been ill. If not for her family, Junie knew she might not have made it through. More than once, she'd thought of following Mark to the other side.

Thank goodness she hadn't.

Jo's cheery voice broke into her thoughts. "You're working at the hotel gift shop now and making friends there. And I saw you at Cuppa Jo's. Blue introduced you to everyone. You don't have to be alone if you don't want to be."

"I don't know…"

Jo smiled with confidence. "Sunshine Avenue is a great street. We often pool our suppers for potluck on the spur of the moment or share a bottle of wine at sunset. You'd love it here."

Junie stared back at the sad, decrepit house. She knew it was time she faced the last of her fears. Drawing a nervous breath, she said, "Maybe this old house and I are meant for each other."

Jo's eyes widened. "Does that mean you'll buy it?"

At her friend's stark words, Junie suddenly realized the

magnitude of this step. She wasn't just renting a place but taking full responsibility for it—repairs and all. Still, the price was right. So was the location. Doubts surged through her mind, and she held up her hand.

"Not yet." Junie shook her head. "First, I need to talk to my mom about this. And my grandmother. She knows the island so well."

"Okay, but please don't wait too long," Jo said, frowning. "I'm not the only person who knows this house is going up for sale—and probably for a higher price than the heirs would entertain right now. I really want you to be a part of Sunshine Avenue."

"I appreciate that," Junie said, smiling. She had only known Jo a few months, but they'd become good friends. "Thanks for showing me, and I promise I'll think about it." Junie swung into the golf cart. "Shall I drop you off at the diner?"

"Sure," Jo replied. "And I won't tell anyone else about this place until you decide. But I have a strong feeling it's going to sell quickly. Houses like this don't come along every day."

"I know." Neither did men like Mark.

While Junie needed to move, especially given Maileah's temperament, she wasn't sure if she was truly ready to live on her own. More than being alone, she feared regressing into that dark place she'd been. What if she made a mistake?

AFTER DROPPING off Jo at her restaurant, Junie wheeled the golf cart back to the Majestic Hotel, the old Victorian-era hotel that was the pride of Crown Island. She parked in the employee area before hurrying toward the gift shop. Her phone buzzed, and she glanced down as she walked. It was Jo, telling her she overheard someone at Cuppa Jo's talking about the house on Sunshine Avenue.

Don't take too long to think about it.

Surprised at that, Junie rounded a corner in the shopping corridor with her head down, still focusing on the message.

A tall, solid man cried out just as they made contact, and a sheaf of papers took flight, fluttering down around them. She stumbled back in surprise, her arms flailing.

"Got you," he cried, catching her by the arm. His firm grip kept her from falling, but her phone lurched away.

He caught it with his free hand. "And your phone, too."

"I'm sorry I didn't see you," she said, embarrassed at her clumsiness.

"It's okay. I've done the same thing." He held out her phone like a prize.

Only then did Junie look up at the man who'd caught her. His warm, greenish-hazel eyes were filled with amusement. His firm grip on her arm relaxed, though his hand lingered for a moment, magnetic in its touch. Dark auburn hair curled just beneath his earlobes. He was large and well-built, like some sort of legendary Scottish Highlander.

Or maybe she's been watching too many *Outlander* episodes in the dark of her room. She should have stepped back more quickly than she did, but she was strangely rooted to the spot—and to him.

"Uh, thanks," Junie managed to say. His actions were impressively swift. "How did you catch that? My phone, I mean."

"I'm good with my hands." The man gave her a nod,

then continued on his way. He glanced back to give her a half-grin.

Junie smiled at him, feeling mildly embarrassed. Her friend Jo was right about people on Crown Island. She wondered if that guy was a local or a hotel guest.

Not that it mattered, she thought, recovering from the encounter. But wow, she'd never met anyone like him before. If Maileah were here, she'd be after him in a heartbeat.

As Junie unlocked the door, she flipped over the sign that read, *Gone to the Beach*, turning it to *We're Open, Sunshine*. She waved to Faye, the neighboring owner of The Body Boutique, and went inside.

A hotel guest in shorts and sandals followed her and began browsing her selection of sea-inspired candles. "It smells wonderful in here," the woman said.

"That's the new Ocean Air candle," Junie said, pointing toward a blue box.

The woman brought it to her nose and inhaled. A smile warmed her face. "I'll need several of these."

"I have plenty." While the woman shopped, Junie gathered several of the candles from her backstock before turning her attention to the bookkeeping.

Her shop sales were climbing, much to the hotel manager's surprise. Like the house on Sunshine Avenue, this shop had been a disaster when she'd first seen it, although not nearly as bad. Whitley, who had managed the hotel for years, had given her a chance to show him what she could do with it. He was pleased with her efforts, as was the new hotel owner, Ryan Kingston.

Ryan and her mother were seeing a lot of each other, and Junie was trying to adjust to the idea of her mother dating. Fortunately, Junie had landed this position on her own before her mother and Ryan started going out.

This was the first job Junie had attempted since Mark died. She sold the online shop they'd built together. That had started with athletic shoes and expanded into athleisure fashion. Junie had done all the buying and created the assortment and visuals. She'd loved doing that, but she'd lost the heart to go on after her husband's death.

Now, she was feeling better and enjoying the fresh challenge, thanks to this store.

While some people might have seen a tired old gift shop, Junie saw an opportunity. With her entrepreneurial inclination awakened, she dove in.

First, she made drastic markdowns on the old inventory. She sold it all and donated the rest. Next, she cleaned the space, repurposed vintage fixtures, and re-merchandised the entire store. She brought in luxurious Majestic-branded merchandise and unusual local crafts. Most of her new assortment sold well.

Now, she wanted to expand the offerings with unique products of her own. And that would change her original plan.

Junie and her husband had owned a profitable online store, so she was confident in her merchandising and online marketing skills. While her husband's life insurance and the sale of their online store left her without financial concerns, she didn't want to make any mistakes. Not in buying an old house or in building another company. This time, she had to make those decisions on her own, which was slightly terrifying but also exciting.

She was more confident about a new product line venture. In fact, she had an idea she wanted to discuss with

Whitley and Ryan. If they would allow it, she would have exactly what she wanted.

If not, she didn't know how long she'd be satisfied working in a hotel gift shop.

In that regard, her sister had been right. Maileah, who had worked in marketing for a technology company in Seattle before being laid off, insisted that Junie was working far beneath her pay grade. That was true, but Junie had needed this.

And now, her entrepreneurial curiosity was awakened, and she yearned for more.

A man in a police officer's uniform stepped inside. He was attractive enough to have been included on this year's Crown Island fundraising calendar featuring the men and women of the community's police force and firefighting force—*Serving the Crown*, it was called. Blue was even featured on the cover of the calendar, which she'd seen in her friend Faye's shop across the hall.

"Hi, Junie. Thought I'd stop by to see how you're doing. I saw you drop off Jo a little earlier."

Junie greeted him with an air kiss to the cheek. "Nothing gets past you, Blue." She counted him as a new friend. They'd gone to an evening jam session at Cuppa Jo's not long ago, where she'd met many locals.

"That's my job."

She noticed tiny beads of perspiration on his broad forehead, though it was pleasantly cool inside. "Is there something I can help you with, Blue?"

Hesitating, Blue tucked a thumb into his belt loop and hitched his trousers before he spoke. "I was thinking, that is, if you're available, maybe you'd like to see the Beach

Festival fireworks show on Friday. It's a local event that celebrates the founding of Crown Island."

"Sure, who's going?"

"Most everyone, I guess." He rubbed his neck as if uncomfortable. "But I thought, well, maybe you'd like to have dinner with me before we go?"

He seemed nervous, and Junie's senses went on alert. This sounded different from their casual evening at Cuppa Jo's. He'd simply given her a ride and introduced her to others. She didn't count that as a date. Or was it?

"By ourselves?" she managed to squeak out. She hadn't been on a date since Mark died. Even the thought of dating seemed so far away.

Blue stroked his chin. "Sure, just us. If you want to, I mean."

The hotel guest was standing behind Blue with several candles. With relief, Junie quickly motioned her to the register. "Excuse me, Officer Blumenthal. I need to ring up this guest."

He stepped aside, and the woman placed the candles she'd selected on the vintage table that served as a checkout counter.

"These are our most popular candles, and the aroma is fabulous," Junie said to the woman. "Be sure to trim the wick a little each time so that it doesn't char the inside of the container. I visited the artisan creators recently, too. Why, you should see the care they take in making these by hand."

Junie chatted with the guest, rattling off more instructions and talking about the candlemakers. The woman was talkative, too. Junie was thankful for that because she had no idea how to respond to Blue.

Had she misled him? He was very nice, but he wasn't anything like Mark.

No one was, though,

Taking her time to calm her nerves, Junie carefully wrapped each candle individually. Using one of her special gift bags, she created a lovely presentation, even though the woman was only going back to her room. The woman seemed amused and kept glancing between Junie and Blue with a smile.

Junie didn't know what to do. She enjoyed Blue's company when he stopped by the shop to chat, but she hadn't thought of him beyond that.

Still, if she wanted the chance to start a family someday, a father would likely be part of that equation unless she got creative. And she had no idea how to do that, either. Maybe she could adopt a child as a single woman, but she had always envisioned herself being happily married with children. To Mark, or even someone like that man she'd nearly knocked over, she mused. She shook her head. Wherever that thought came from.

Maileah would surely laugh at her for that.

But Blue was here now. And he was waiting for her. Each time she stole a glance at him, her chest tightened with trepidation.

When Junie finished affixing every embellishment she could think of to the woman's package—bows and streamers, handfuls of fluffy pink tissue, clip-on mermaids and starfish, a sticker with the name of the shop, another one for the Majestic Hotel, even a little votive candle in another scent as a gift, plus her business card and coupon for another visit—she looked up.

"Will there be anything else?" she asked hopefully. "Any

other gifts you might need? Or something to pamper yourself? We have matching room sprays…"

The woman chuckled. "This is beautiful—and it's quite enough." She paused, whispering, "Besides, I think someone is expecting an answer."

Junie's face blazed, and she wanted to crawl under the table. She knew her face flushed bright red with embarrassment—she'd been teased about that all her life. She thanked the guest, and the woman strolled out, waggling her eyebrows.

With any luck, the fire alarm would go off, an earthquake would rattle the windows, or the Loch Ness creature's seafaring cousin would spring to the beach and gobble them whole. She stared at the table, praying for disaster to strike, but fortune betrayed her.

Blue shifted from one foot to another. "Junie, what do you think about the fireworks? And dinner?"

"I think we're both sort of nervous," she replied, rubbing her cheek.

He let out a whoosh of relief. "I don't do this very often. Ask out people, I mean. Women, that is." He coughed and flushed as he stumbled over his words.

Blue was good-looking and capable—straight out of Central Casting, as her mother once said. Junie wouldn't have expected him to be so awkward, so it was sort of endearing.

She gave him a small, empathetic smile. "I understand. And if you're wondering, I haven't gone out with anyone since Mark."

A horrified look crossed his face. "Oh, my gosh, I didn't think about that. If you're not ready…"

Junie blinked at a length of ribbon she'd twisted into

knots, just like her stomach. If she never took a chance, she would never know what might develop in her future. She had to start somewhere. And yet— The ribbon snapped. "Can I let you know tomorrow?"

"Sure," Blue said, sounding relieved. "You can text me."

"I don't have your number."

"Oh, right. I can put it in your phone."

"Just write it down." Junie fumbled for a pad of paper and slid it across the table.

Blue scribbled his number. "See you around. Or by text. Or maybe tomorrow."

"I'll be here," she said, her voice squeaking again. Her chirpiness was grating even to her ears. "Or I'll call you."

"Or text, huh?"

Junie twisted the ribbon tighter. "Right. Or text."

"Sure. Okay. Sounds good." He backed out of the door and hurried away.

Junie sank her face into her hands. What would her mother or Jo have to say about that tongue-twisted exchange?

Or Maileah? She winced at the thought of that. Her sister had men panting after her.

The house on Sunshine Avenue and her idea for a new line were enough to think about. She certainly didn't need a man in her life.

She squeezed her eyes shut. Unless it were Mark.

But that was only wishful thinking.

2

*J*unie was in the storeroom replenishing candles when she heard someone walk into the gift shop. She hurried out and was delighted to see her grandmother. Ella had been ill for months, so Junie was relieved to see her strong enough to go out again.

"Hello, my darling." Ella greeted her with an embrace.

Junie expected to see her mother or Maileah with her. "Nana, are you here by yourself?"

"I am perfectly capable of managing on my own, you know."

Junie worried about her grandmother, yet today, she did look well. Her face glowed against the rose-colored lace dress she wore. "Are you sure?"

"I'm quite capable of assessing my physical health." Ella's eyes glittered with determination.

Her grandmother had worked as an emergency room nurse at the small hospital she and her late husband had helped establish on Crown Island. Most residents knew Ella and Dr. Augustus Raines.

"Isn't it time for your coffee break?" Ella asked. "I'm famished for a carrot cake I saw at the bakery. And I dressed for the occasion."

Her grandmother looked nice in a soft spring dress and pearls.

"Let's go." Junie flipped the sign on the door.

As they walked to the beachside bakery cafe at the hotel, several people stopped them to greet Ella, who hadn't been out much after a long bout with pneumonia had left her weak. When they arrived at the cafe, the host greeted Junie and seated them at a prime table on the sunny terrace under a marine-blue umbrella. A light ocean breeze fluttered the white tablecloth.

The general manager approached them and stopped before her grandmother. Clasping Ella's hands, Whitley smiled. "It's awfully good to see you."

"And you as well," Ella said, holding his gaze before taking in his vivid turquoise jacket. "This color is perfect on you," she added. "Of course, you always look so stylish."

"Coming for you, that's a high compliment, indeed," Whitley said. "You're looking extraordinarily well. And lovely as always."

Junie could almost feel the sparks sizzling between them as they spoke. She'd also noticed their sparkle at the VIP reception Ryan Kingston had organized to meet the local community. Or maybe it was only the familiarity of old friendship. She could hardly imagine Ella dating.

Dating. Junie winced at the thought. If only she'd had the foresight to freeze her eggs or Mark's sperm or whatever people who never planned to have another relationship did. She wished she had known about that.

"I almost envy my granddaughter working here at the hotel," Ella said to Whitley.

"Junie is doing a fine job." Whitley dragged his gaze from Ella and turned to Junie. "Your new merchandising assortment is quite promising."

"Sales are steadily increasing," Junie replied, wresting her thoughts back from the brink. Deciding to take a chance, she added, "I have an idea I'd like to talk with you about later."

Whitley raised his brow with interest. "I'd like to hear it. You've done well turning the gift shop around. That was more than we expected."

Junie wasn't sure he'd feel the same after she shared her plan with him. "I'll get on your schedule." This wouldn't be a casual conversation, so she wanted his full attention.

Whitley nodded toward a server for them. "I must excuse myself. I hope to see more of you here, Ella." Taking her hand, he executed a whisper of a kiss above her skin.

Her grandmother beamed. "You can count on that. After all, this is my favorite place on Crown Island."

Junie could have sworn she saw a flush rise in Whitley's face, but he recovered quickly and moved on.

Junie turned back to her grandmother. "Whitley seems to have special affection for you, Nana."

"I'm sure he treats all the women the same," Ella said. "He's so gracious.

"I'm sure he doesn't." Junie hadn't seen Whitley treat anyone like he did her grandmother. He was cordial and welcoming to others, but he had a special spark in his eyes for her nana.

Ella noted that with the slightest lift of her brow, but she brushed away the idea with a small wave.

Junie wondered if they might have unspoken feelings for each other. She walked a couple of fingers toward her grandmother's hand and tapped it. "I think Whitley likes you."

Ella angled her chin. "We're old friends."

"Maybe it's not too late to see where that takes you."

"Why, Junie. You surprise me. And what about you?"

Junie shook her head. "I'm too old for that." That's how she felt, not her chronological age.

A smile danced on Ella's lips. "When you're older, you might feel younger. Life is funny that way." Her gaze drifted across the room to Whitley.

Junie caught that. Had she planted an idea in her grandmother's mind, or had it been there all along?

Ella clutched her hand. "Enough of this. Let's have something marvelous."

When the server arrived at the table, Ella ordered the carrot cake she'd had her eye on, and Junie opted for a chocolate croissant with mocha coffee.

"Chocolate is my weakness," Junie said.

"It's proven to lift the spirits." Ella rested her chin in her hand. "That means chocolate is therapy for whatever is troubling you."

Junie definitely needed that; she wasn't sure which way her life was going right now. But she wasn't sure how to verbalize it.

Averting her eyes from Ella's inquisitive gaze, Junie tented her hand to her forehead against the sun and looked out toward the sea where a fishing vessel trolled on the horizon. A young mother with three stairstep-aged children ventured near the waves. Retired couples and young couples alike strolled the beach holding hands. A few digital nomads tapped on laptops or tablets under umbrellas. They all seemed to have a purpose.

What was hers now?

Ella sat back and nodded toward a group of girls who looked to be about twelve years old. Their laughter and giggles punctuated the rhythmic sound of the waves. Lifeguards watched over them all.

"They remind me of you and Maileah and your friends at that age," Ella said. "You could play for hours and hours."

Recalling her childhood summers at this beach, Junie sighed. "Everything seemed so simple then."

"How is your life so complicated now?"

Her grandmother always knew when something was weighing on her mind. Junie plunged in. "I saw a house on Sunshine Avenue. I'm thinking about buying it." At least, that was something she could control.

Ella broke into a smile. "Why, that's wonderful, honey. Which one is it?"

"It's the worst house on the street," Junie replied, wrinkling her nose as she recalled the stench. "It's been a rental property for a little while, and it's awfully rundown. Jo lives across the street, and she told me it's coming up for sale. She said it used to be a sweet little cottage, and she thinks it can be again."

Ella put a finger to her chin. "If it's the one with an orchard next to it, that was once quite nice. The Ashbury family lived there. What are they asking for it?"

Junie repeated what Jo had told her, and her grandmother pressed her lips together, considering. "That sounds fair, and you have that tucked away in your investment account, don't you?"

"I could pay cash and still have plenty to make repairs. That account has gone up about thirty percent in the two years since Mark died. I've hardly touched it." Junie hesitated before she shared her deepest concern. "That's part of the problem. I think of that as Mark's money, and I wonder if he'd be happy with the house."

Ella tilted her head in empathy. "Mark was a wonderful, responsible man, so I'm sure he'd want you to have a home and be close to your family. And I couldn't be happier knowing you're so close."

Junie knew that would make her grandmother happy. Still, she swallowed hard against her memories. "The house would seem empty, though, knowing that Mark should have been there with me. We always talked about buying our first home when I got pregnant. We were trying to start a family when he…" Junie sucked in a small breath. *Stepped in front of a taxi that ran a light in London*, she finished in her mind. "The future I thought was mine was ripped away in an instant."

Ella clasped her hand. "Your life can change again in an instant—only this time, for the better. Nothing in life is guaranteed. The question is, are you ready to take another chance?"

"You're so optimistic," Junie said, smiling. She loved that about her grandmother.

"And why not?" Ella spread her hand toward people on the beach. "You could bump into someone tomorrow who might change the course of your life."

As her grandmother spoke, Junie spied the man she had collided with at the hotel. He was walking past the cafe. Her heart skipped as she watched him. He was attractive enough, but he was also a guest who would probably be gone tomorrow.

"Doubtful," Junie said as she averted her eyes. When her grandmother looked surprised, she quickly added, "But it's a nice thought."

For some reason, she felt a little guilty about how she'd felt in that brief encounter, especially after talking about Mark. Still, that man was a complete stranger.

A small smile grew on Ella's face. "Then again, some friendships develop over time into something more lasting."

"Like Whitley?"

Ella dipped her chin. "I was referring to Blue. I saw him leave the boutique. Didn't you have a nice time with him at Cuppa Jo's?"

"That wasn't a date." Junie twisted her lips to one side as she considered that. Her heart wasn't involved at all when she thought about Blue.

"Are you sure he didn't think it was?"

Junie wasn't. "It was more like a friendship thing." She paused. "Actually, he asked me out for dinner before the fireworks this weekend."

Ella's eyes brightened. "It's good for you to get out."

Junie heard a certain nonchalance in her grandmother's voice. "I'm not sure how to answer him. Did you know anything about this, Nana?"

"Not this time." Ella smiled. "But do you like him?"

"He's more of a friend." Junie ran a hand across her brow. She needed her grandmother's perspective. "With Mark, I liked him from the very beginning. The instant we met. But I know some people start out as friends. What do you think?"

"I believe there's no harm in going out with him if you feel comfortable. Couples start their relationships in different ways. It's where they end up that counts."

Just then, Sailor sauntered toward them. With his blond ponytail, T-shirt, and beach shorts, his look couldn't be farther away from Blue's clean-cut style. Mark's had been somewhere in between.

Sailor greeted Ella first, then turned to Junie. "Hey, I just stopped by the gift shop and saw that it was closed."

"You found me," Junie said. "What's up, Sailor?"

"Want to go to the fireworks with me this weekend? We could go to Cuppa Jo's for a burger before."

Junie sat back, stunned. Another date? Sailor was so casual about it, unlike Blue. "I think I might have plans. Can I let you know?"

"Sure, that's cool. Hey, I've got a couple of openings for the surf training you were asking about on the day you wanted. Want me to count you in?"

"I don't know…" Junie was afraid of getting too far out in the ocean.

"Why, that sounds like such fun," Ella said. "You should take Maileah, too."

Her sister was still feeling sorry for herself. While her boyfriend had cheated on her, he'd also done her a favor. Junie still couldn't believe what Hawk had done—and with their father's girlfriend. She shuddered. Fiancé, that is. She was hoping that was one wedding that wouldn't come to pass.

Sailor was waiting for an answer. "Two, then?"

"I can't believe I'm saying this, but yes." Junie shook her head in amazement at herself. "Do I need a board?"

"I have everything you need."

Was that a double entendre? Junie wondered, but Sailor seemed oblivious. He wore a happy-go-lucky grin. Was it the endorphins surfing released or the dollop of Vitamin D the sunshine served up?

"I'll see you guys soon." Sailor headed off to open the bike rental concession he ran at the hotel.

A smile lifted the corner of Ella's mouth. "Looks like you have a variety of options now."

Julie lowered her voice. "Blue was so nervous he could hardly get his words out."

"Sailor is certainly confident," Ella replied, leaning in. "And they're both nice men. Blue is, well, somewhat complicated, but then, one might expect that given his profession."

Her grandmother knew both men better than she did. "And what about Sailor? He's always so happy and nonchalant. Doesn't anything bother him?"

"He's a natural champion—surfing the waves, of course, but also a champion of children. I'd like to see Sailor get a real break in surfing."

Junie hadn't thought of Sailor that way, but then she'd only seen him at the bike rental concession and at Cuppa Jo's. "Does he work with kids on Crown Island?"

"At the beach, often after school, and in the summer." Ella pointed to a spot on the beach. "Right over there, where you'll meet for lessons. Watch him with the children sometime."

Junie liked men who were good with kids. She should probably have a checklist, as some of her single friends did, but she hated thinking about dating like that. She didn't like thinking about dating at all, but here she was. She shook her head.

As if reading her mind, Ella said, "Think of dates as making friends first. That might not be so intimidating."

"I wouldn't want to mislead them."

"This is a small island, and they're adults. Even if Sailor doesn't act like one. Be honest with them that you're easing into dating."

"I'm not sure I'll have time," Junie said. "If I buy that house, I'll be busy. Maybe I could get a dog. Or a cat. That might be enough."

Ella only raised an eyebrow.

The server delivered their cake and croissant, and while they ate, Junie chatted with her grandmother about the daunting new landscape of her life.

Still, Junie wanted a family, whatever that might look like. Despite Ella's advice, maybe it was time to go all in on her future, like a cold plunge in an icy pool.

3

*A*pril folded the blue canvas sleeper sofa she'd bought for her mother by pressing down on the frame and sliding it back into position. With Maileah in the guest room and Junie in April's old room, they were all crammed into Ella's bungalow on Beach View Lane.

As she replaced the cushions, she smiled in satisfaction. She loved her children and her mother, and she wouldn't have it any other way.

Maileah and Junie were currently arguing in the bathroom, just as they had as children.

Nevertheless, April loved having her girls on Crown Island, where she'd grown up. Junie was starting over, and Maileah was safe from her dangerous ex-boyfriend in Seattle. And neither one of them was speaking to their father.

April couldn't blame them. Not that he cared; he was busy with his new girlfriend. While the love and admiration she'd once had for Calvin was long gone, he was still her daughters' father. Shame on him for neglecting them through this transition. He should have been reassuring them of his love for them instead of hiding out in an alternate life.

She brushed her hands on her old, faded jeans as if to sweep away those irritating thoughts.

"Good morning," Ella said, walking into the living room. "You look like you're ready for a workday. Still cleaning the new space?"

"The crew I hired did an incredible job." Converting the old space that backed up to the Majestic Hotel for her Crown Island Historical Society was a much larger undertaking than April had realized. "Today I'm meeting Deb. She's bringing her crew to open the front and add larger windows and pocket doors."

April had spent the last few months drawing up plans with Deb, rallying support for the new historical society, and raising funds to fulfill her vision and service to the community. Ryan had even donated the Princess Noelle necklace Junie discovered in her storeroom. She planned to auction it, with all proceeds to fund the society.

"Sounds like a big job."

"Deb assures me it will go smoothly." April noted her mother's smart navy blouse and white skirt. "You look nice. Going out again?"

"I'm meeting friends from City Hall for coffee, then joining others from the hospital for lunch."

"Aren't you the social butterfly now? I hope you don't overdo it."

Ella lifted her chin. "I know how to pace myself."

April thought her mother looked well now, though Ella had given them all a fright last summer with her illness.

A knock sounded at the door, and Ella opened it to the mail carrier. "Hello, Lynette. Have something for me?"

"A package, along with the rest of your mail. Have a good day, Ella."

"What's that?" April asked.

"Just a little gift I ordered for a friend." Ella placed the small package on the counter and thumbed through the envelopes. Two large, creamy envelopes were on the bottom. "Impressive," Ella said. "These look like wedding invitations. They're for Junie and Maileah."

April arranged the accent cushions on the couch. "Maybe one of their friends from the neighborhood in Seattle is getting married. Who are they from?"

Ella turned over an envelope and sucked in a soft breath. "Oh, dear."

"What's wrong?" Junie asked as she entered the room with Maileah right behind her.

"Good morning, girls. You just received some wedding invitations."

Ella gave April an odd, almost apologetic look and handed the envelopes to her granddaughters. "See for yourself."

Junie turned the envelope over. "This is weird. It's our old address—I mean, Dad's address."

"Don't open that." Maileah snatched the envelope and turned away.

"Oh, no, you don't," Junie said, grabbing her sister's hoodie and plucking the envelope from her hands. Sliding her finger under the thick flap, she pulled out the invitation. Her mouth opened in shock. "What the—"

"I tried to warn you," Maileah replied, looking guilty.

A chill coursed through April. Instantly, she knew. "Your father's wedding?"

Maileah's eyes rounded. "Mom, I'm so sorry."

Junie whirled around. "Have you been talking to Dad and what's her name again?"

"No," Maileah replied, drawing out the word in a plaintive wail. "I guess I saw a post on social media."

"I haven't even received the final divorce papers," April said numbly, though they had been legally separated for months. The courts had been slow over the holidays. Still, she would not allow this to shade her mood. She lifted her chin. "I suppose he might as well get on with his life. I certainly am."

Junie marched into the kitchen, lit a match, and touched it to the invitation. As it curled into the flames, she tossed it into the sink with a satisfied smirk. "Why would he think we have any interest in going? We are *not* one big happy family. He saw to that." She glared at Maileah. "You knew about this, didn't you?"

Maileah heaved a guilty sigh. "Olga texted me, but I didn't respond."

Junie jerked the other invitation from her sister's frozen grip and tossed it aside. "You're not going either."

"I never want to see him, or her, again." Maileah pressed her lips together. "We don't have to go, do we, Mom?"

April hated that her daughters had to go through this. After what Calvin had done, why would he invite them to his wedding? He was just as self-centered as always. With a glance at her mother, she spoke as calmly as she could. "You two are free to do whatever you want. He's your father."

It was all she could do to hold back how she really felt. She'd moved on, but still, Calvin had hurt her. More than that, he'd hurt her daughters, and she would have done anything to avoid seeing the looks on their faces now.

Ella nodded her approval. "Given the circumstances, you don't have to attend."

Maileah was doubly damaged. Olga had a fling with her boyfriend. That could have been Calvin's out, but he forged ahead, stubborn man in need of validation that he was.

April blew out a breath—and forced out her animosity with it. *Just breathe*, she told herself. She picked up her purse and opened the front door. "I'll see you all later."

Once she was outside, she gulped fresh ocean air to quell her nerves. While she was over Calvin, what he was doing to their daughters infuriated her. She fought the urge to call him. Yet, Junie and Maileah didn't need her inter-vention. They were adults and capable of handling this, although she would be there to listen as needed.

A dusty silver Land Rover pulled to the curb, and April held up her hand in greeting. Years ago, Deb had bought this second-hand SUV to haul pieces for her interior design business.

"Hope I didn't keep you waiting," Deb said as April climbed in.

"You won't believe what just happened." When April told her, Deb just shook her head.

"Calvin deserves what he's going to get in that marriage," Deb said. "Olga will crush him. Thank good-ness the divorce is nearly over. Have you received the final documents?"

"Today, I hope." April saw Ryan pulling from his driveway at the end of the street. "Slow down. I want to talk to him."

Deb grinned. "You've sure upgraded from Calvin."

When Ryan saw her, he rolled down his window. "Hi, hon. Where are you headed?"

"To work on the historical society office with Deb." At the sight of Ryan, April's heart quickened. The morning sun illuminated his blue eyes and glistened off his dark hair. She recalled the day she'd surprised him by trespassing in his garden. He'd just stepped out of the shower. Even now, that pleasant vision was firmly lodged in her memory.

Yes, she had upgraded, she thought happily.

Ryan rested a hand on the steering wheel and grinned. "Want to join me for lunch at the Majestic? There's someone I'd like for you to meet. A new team member. If he accepts my offer."

April shook her head. "I'll be a mess by then. Can we do it over dinner?"

"Sure. I'll invite the guy to the house. And I'll bring lunch to you two. I know what you like." He blew her a kiss and drove away.

Deb watched him go. "Wow. Where do I find another one like that?"

April smiled. Deb had never married, though she dated a lot. "I wonder who he wants me to meet?"

"Please let it be his long-lost single brother." Deb grinned. "But seriously, how's it going with Ryan?"

"Pretty good, except he wants me to spend more time at his place."

"And what's wrong with that?"

"How would that look to the girls? Especially after what their father is doing."

Deb twirled a strand of her blond hair. "You're divorced, not dead."

"I want to take this relationship slowly. I dove into the last one and look what happened."

"Ryan is not Calvin," Deb said.

"Thank goodness. But I want to be sure."

As Deb turned a corner onto Orange Avenue, she nodded. "I respect that. If I took my time, I wouldn't have all these scars on my heart. But then, I wouldn't have had nearly as much fun."

April laughed. Deb had certainly had her share of boyfriends. She was quick to jump into relationships and just as quick to leave when they no longer suited her.

They neared the location. A group of men in work garb were waiting near the front in their pickup trucks. "Is that your crew?"

"Sure is," Deb replied. "Let's get to work."

April stepped from the SUV and opened the front door to the old structure, which had once been a dance hall adjacent to the Majestic Hotel. She had learned this building was built a few years after the main hotel and before the turn of the century, making it more than a hundred years old. Likely, it was built to handle increased demand during the hotel's heyday. The Majestic was one of the world's largest wooden Victorian structures, designed by the same team of architects responsible for the Hotel Del Coronado on nearby Coronado Island.

Ryan's acquisition of the old hotel had made the news and brought him back to his hometown. He had grown up in a different part of the small town; he was the son of a janitor and housekeeper at the hotel and had a brilliant investment career before returning. They had only recently met. How fast life could change, she thought.

"Ready for the demolition?" Deb asked.

April twisted her mouth to one side as she surveyed the equipment the men had brought. "Maybe I should have waited on that cleaning."

"Life gets messy," Deb said. "My team will seal off the front area so you can work in the rear. Though it will be noisy."

Just then, April's phone dinged with a message. It was from her attorney. *Good news. You're a free woman now.*

April smiled and showed the message to Deb, who flung her arms around her. "You're free now. How does it feel?"

"It seems anti-climactic. But good riddance." April turned back to the building, refocusing on the task at hand. Even though there had been many good times, the past was behind her now. Her future was here on Crown Island, and it would be what she would make of it. She wished the same for her daughters, too.

"Let's do this," April said, giving Deb a high-five.

By NOON, April was invigorated by the progress Deb's team was making. The small, old windows in the front were gone, and the crew was busy enlarging the opening and repairing the existing wooden frame that was now exposed. Deb had suggested sliding, pocket-style doors that would open the entire space to the sidewalk to draw in visitors. With the mild year-round weather on Crown Island, most shops and cafes opened onto the wide sidewalks.

Behind the heavy plastic the workers had put up, April and Deb worked on the layout of the shop. The old wooden dance floor was staying, as was the beamed ceiling. Using the services of an electrician, April and Deb determined the placement of ceiling fans and new lighting.

After the contractor left, Deb unveiled her new design concepts, showing April color swatches and paint chips on a vision board.

April was surprised at the extent of work that her friend had put in. "You didn't have to do all of this."

"This is the fun part for me," Deb said. "Besides, this place isn't only for you. The historical society benefits all of Crown Island."

April nodded. "That's the plan."

She already had a variety of events scheduled. She had lined up volunteers for everything from city walking tours to a new garden committee. Residents would open their gardens to the community and raise funds through ticket sales. Part of the funds would be returned to the historical society. The other part would be used to preserve existing common spaces and add new plants, trees, and flowers to the local park and other areas.

April inspected Deb's images and sketches. "I don't think we need these sorts of furnishings here. They look expensive. I'd planned on using second-hand pieces, maybe with some history attached."

"You'll still need a few pieces. I can get a lot of the cost covered through donations. I have friends with furniture shops who often donate furnishings from prior seasons."

Even so, it was more than April had imagined. "I appreciate that, but you've already donated a lot of your time."

Deb raised her brow. "You're like my sister. I'm here to help however I can. And Crown Island is my community, too."

April hugged her. "I don't know what I'd do without you."

"I'm sure you'd manage," Deb said. "You always did have a knack for managing the near impossible."

"Are you referring to my marriage? If so, I did that for the girls. And Calvin was an expert at duplicity, although, in the last few years, he got sloppy."

"I wasn't referring to that." Deb leveled a gaze at her. "We must celebrate your divorce today. Get rid of that baggage and move on."

Laughing lightly, April said, "Since he's sending out wedding invitations, I should think so."

"Then it's settled. This afternoon, I can watch over the work here while you clean up. Champagne at the Majestic?"

"You're the best." April hugged her friend. She would have dinner with Ryan later.

Just then, the rear door nearest to the Majestic opened, and Ryan walked in with box lunches in hand.

"Ready for a break?" he asked, holding up the lunches.

"We sure are," April replied. The difference between Ryan and Calvin couldn't be starker.

Ryan turned and motioned to someone behind him. In whisked a server with a folding table and chairs, and another one with flowers and table settings.

Holding out his arms, Ryan said, "If you can't break for lunch at the Majestic, then the Majestic will come to you."

Deb bumped April on the shoulder. "I think he's a keeper."

"Thank you, darling." April touched his cheek, her heart tightening at this beautiful man's thoughtfulness. It wasn't for show or accolades from her friend; Ryan was always thoughtful. *So unlike what's his name.*

The three of them sat down to a lovely meal of assorted

salads, crusty bread, and tomato basil soup drizzled with truffle oil. Deb discussed the exterior renovation and landscaping on the sides that faced the hotel, which the Majestic was covering. Ryan had agreed to cover the major improvements to the property, although April's new historical society was paying for the upgrades and furnishings.

When they finished, Ryan gave her a brief kiss. "I'll see you for dinner later. I think my new recruit will appreciate your insight on island life."

"I'd like that, and I'll be happy to share," April said, wondering what dinner at Ryan's house would be like. For a man who had lived in hotels much of his adult life, cooking wasn't likely to be one of his talents. Still, he'd surprised her before.

"Hi, everyone," April called out as she walked into her mother's house. She was feeling fine after she and Deb had toasted to her new life with a glass of champagne at the Majestic.

Ella and Junie were seated at the kitchen table. "You two look serious," April said. "What's up?"

"Your daughter is thinking about buying a house," Ella said.

April looked at Junie in surprise. "Here on Crown Island?"

"Not far from here," Junie replied. "The house needs some work, but it comes with plenty of space for a garden."

"Your grandmother and I can help you with that." This was a huge step for Junie, and she was pleased to hear it. "I didn't know you were thinking such a thing."

She glanced over her shoulder and lowered her voice. "I

wasn't…until Maileah arrived. Jo told me about it; she lives across the street. Now that I'm working, I should live like an adult again."

Behind her, Maileah sauntered in, her hair in disarray. She wore a slouchy sweatshirt and torn denim shorts. "Was that a dig about me?"

"Not at all," Junie replied. "You've been telling me to get my act together for a long time. Now I am. I thought you'd be happy."

Maileah plopped onto a chair. "A real house. Imagine that." She heaved a sigh. "Before I got laid off, I was planning on buying a condo in Seattle with what's his name."

"I suppose that wasn't meant to be," Ella said, clasping Maileah's hand. "Life zigs and zags, and we each get our turn. You're due for a break, dear. You simply need to get back out there."

April knew that was easier to say than do, especially for Maileah, who seemed depressed. She hugged Junie. "I'd love to hear more about your plans, but I'm due at Ryan's for dinner. He wants me to meet a potential new member of his management team. I think a house sounds like a grand idea, sweetie. And Maileah, your turn will come around again."

"I don't know how it will here on Crown Island," Maileah said, sounding dejected. "I should be back in Seattle. But I'm not getting any calls on my resume."

"We'll talk about your options." Ella cast a look at April behind Maileah's back.

Maileah had always been April's problem child. She was smart and fun-loving, but she was also mercurial and had astoundingly poor judgment at times. Like when she befriended her father's mistress, who cheated on both him and Maileah with Maileah's boyfriend. Being let go from her job the same day didn't help. At least Maileah had somewhere to go, and that was here. It was a tight fit, but they were together.

If Junie bought a home, that might spur Maileah to action.

4

*A*fter quickly changing into a spring sundress with a lightweight wrap, April walked the short distance down Beach View Lane to Ryan's stark, modern white house on the corner facing the beach. On a street of colorfully painted houses, his stood out. Too much so for the artist colony of Crown Island. Chic, but out of place here.

"The door is open," Ryan called out.

April stepped inside. He'd seen her through the wide plate glass windows that should have looked out on the expansive ocean view, but now only faced the plain white wall that surrounded his huge property. She wound her way through the beige and white living room.

She found him in the spotless kitchen with a wooden center island. It didn't look like he'd been cooking, but something smelled delicious. He held a bottle of wine.

"You need more color in your life," April said, smiling.

Ryan looked up. "Fortunately, I have a red wine. Or shall we call it crimson?"

He encircled her with one arm and brushed his lips

softly against hers—a small, yet endearing gesture that never failed to make her feel cherished. He was muscular, yet he touched her with such tenderness.

"I'm serious. Even Ella thinks you should paint your house." April had some ideas, too.

"When the time is right. Right now, the Majestic needs my full attention." Ryan eyed the clock before opening the oven. "The lasagna is almost ready."

"Did you make that?"

He ran a hand through his thick, dark hair. "I read the manual and turned on the oven."

April laughed. "I thought the kitchen looked too clean. Did Gianna make that for you?"

"A built-in chef is one of the perks of owning a hotel," he said, closing the oven door. "Ten minutes to go. Knox should be here soon." He showed her the bottle. "Nice Italian wine."

"One of our favorites. Where is your corkscrew?"

Ryan opened first one drawer and then another. "Thought I had one, but I'll have to improvise."

"I can get one."

Ryan placed his hand on her shoulder and grinned. "I can manage." He plucked a knife from a block stand that looked new.

April slid onto a stool, hoping they wouldn't have to call her mother to dress a wound. "Tell me about your dinner guest before he arrives."

"I've made Knox an offer, so he's considering moving to Crown Island." Ryan worked the cork from the bottle as he spoke. "You know so much about the island."

"So do you."

"Knox has a unique situation, though."

But before Ryan could continue, headlights whisked across the windows. He pulled the cork from the bottle. "He's here."

"I'll get the glasses." April opened a cabinet.

A few moments later, a knock sounded at the front door. "Anyone home?"

"We're in the kitchen," Ryan said.

A younger version of Ryan walked in, yet his hair was a little longer, and a lovely shade of dark ginger. After giving Ryan a friendly bro hug, he looked at April with cautious curiosity.

"Knox, this is April," Ryan began. "She's the one I told you about. A university-level historian and head of the new Crown Island Historical Society. April, meet Knox MacKenzie."

"It's a pleasure to meet you." The younger man had a well-built frame and radiated youthful vitality. With a warm smile, he extended a hand to her.

"Likewise," April said, noting the easy friendship between Ryan and Knox. "Have you been here long?"

"I arrived yesterday," Knox replied. "I'm here for the week to consider Ryan's offer and check out Crown Island."

"Have you ever visited before?" April asked.

"First time," Knox replied.

"Knox worked for me on one of my projects on the East Coast," Ryan explained. "He brought in a tough job on schedule and under budget. With the renovation now underway, I need a good project manager to oversee the Majestic Hotel renovation and continue on the management team. What do you say, Knox?"

"I need to get a feel for Crown Island," Knox replied, easing onto a stool. "It's not just me."

"You're married?" April poured the wine while Ryan brought out the lasagna.

Knox shook his head. "Not anymore, but I have my best girl to think about."

April tried again. "Would that be your…"

"I have a six-year-old daughter," Knox replied. "I'm not sure if moving Penny will be the wisest choice. She likes her school and friends, but she's only in kindergarten. Crown Island is very different from what she's used to. Maybe in a good way." His gaze fell on the lasagna in front of him.

Ryan took off his oven mitts. "Knox's wife disappeared after Penny was born, so he took responsibility for the little one."

Knox brought the wine to his nose, considering it. "I want to make sure I'm making the right decision, both for my career and my daughter."

April felt a wave of empathy for this young man, who didn't look much older than Junie or Maileah. "I think you'll find this community is welcoming and close-knit, almost like an extended family. She would make new friends quickly."

Ryan's hand found hers. He gave it a gentle squeeze that sent a surge of warmth through her. She took it as a silent affirmation.

"What does Penny enjoy doing?" April asked.

"She likes to paint, and she's surprisingly good for a child her age." Knox's face lit up as he spoke. "She's reading and doing well in math, too." He showed them photos on his phone and told them how quickly she caught on and made friends.

"Takes after her father," Ryan said.

April could hear the love and pride in Knox's voice as

he spoke, and it touched her. She told him about activities for children here. "Crown Island is an artist haven, and the schools are well-rated."

"That's what I hear," Knox said. "Anything for the adults?"

"Just about any sort of water sports you'd want," Ryan said. "Surfing, diving, boating, fishing. And there are plenty of people passing through the doors of the Majestic when you want company."

"Crown Island isn't just a physical place," April added. "It's a state of mind, a way of life. A good place for children and families."

"I'll need to find housing for me and my daughter," Knox said. "I also have my parents to consider. They are a huge help with Penny."

April sensed the scales tipping in favor of Crown Island. She looked at Ryan, then back to Knox. "This could be the beginning of a new chapter for your family."

"It might be," Knox said, though he remained noncommittal.

"Let's toast to making that happen," Ryan said. "And dig into this fabulous lasagna."

They moved to a table outside, where they could hear the nearby ocean. Ryan sliced the lasagna while April served the salad. The two men talked about the ongoing renovation project.

April's mind wandered as she enjoyed the evening breeze. She hoped Knox would accept the position Ryan had offered him. She saw few young men of Knox's caliber, and she thought he would be a good addition to the Majestic team.

Knox's position would also take a lot of the burden off

Ryan's shoulders. He'd been wanting to spend more time with her, which she wanted, too, though not at the expense of her daughters, who still needed her. However, Junie's announcement about buying a house was a positive step for her.

As for her and Ryan, April was confident that their time would come. She trusted that Ryan would give her the space and time she needed until then. Still, he'd been single his entire life, and she wondered if he truly understood what he might be getting into with her family.

Junie and Maileah would always be a priority to her, but they would have their own lives, too. Soon, she hoped.

April adjusted her lightweight wrap around her shoulders and cradled her wine. As she thought about Junie, she decided she should look at the house, too. She could tell that her daughter needed a second opinion.

5

*J*unie hesitated at the doorstep of the weathered house on Sunshine Avenue. Her friend Jo slid the key into the old lock again.

"Are you sure about this, sweetie?" April asked, squinting at the peeling paint.

"It's a great location," Junie replied. "Jo lives right across the street in that cute lavender house."

Still, Junie had reservations. Was she truly ready to unlock a new chapter in her life? And was this the right house? She hoped her mother would like it, but she also valued her honest opinion.

"I love living here," Jo added, turning the lock. The door creaked open with what sounded like a sigh of relief.

April peered inside, looking doubtful. "Are you sure it's okay if we go in?"

"The attorney handling Mrs. Ashbury's estate eats breakfast every day at Cuppa Jo's," Junie said. "That's why she trusts Jo to show it to me again."

"I told her all about you," Jo said.

Junie stepped over the threshold. "Has anyone else made an offer yet?"

"Not that I know of, but a lot of people are talking about it. I think the attorney wants to wrap it up soon, and the heirs don't want anything to do with it. Aside from having it cleaned."

"I'm glad they did that," Junie said.

She had been worried about showing the house to her mother in its original state. Now that the surface dirt was gone, the hardwood floors and vintage light fixtures looked nice. Still, the floors would look better refinished. The light fixtures needed a good scrubbing and possibly rewiring.

"I've looked around Crown Island, and I spoke to Deb," Junie said. "She thinks this is a great neighborhood, and it's walking distance to the beach."

April nodded thoughtfully as she gazed around the living room. "This is a charming old house, Junie. Nothing that a little work can't repair, at least in here."

The three of them wandered through the dusty hallways and small bedrooms. Junie could almost hear the laughter and conversations that might have once filled the house.

She peered into the kitchen, imagining it filled with cozy, modern farmhouse decor—and perhaps a splash of color here and there. "I would redo almost everything in here."

"Does it need it?" April asked. She turned the corner and stopped.

Junie stepped into the kitchen. The floor was now yellowed and scuffed. Old wooden cabinetry was worn and grimy.

Jo grinned. "If this doesn't scream 1970s cooking show, I don't know what does."

"You're probably thinking of Julia Child's show," April said. "When I was younger, I once worked with a woman in Summer Beach who knew her quite well. Junie, you remember Ginger Delavie from the Bay family reunion we attended at the Seabreeze Inn."

"I sure do," Junie replied. "She's amazing. Well, if Julia could cook in a place like this, I guess I can, too. For a while, anyway."

Jo laughed, inspecting the avocado-green stove. "The only thing missing is a disco ball."

"And bell-bottom pants," April added.

"Hey, those have come back," Junie said, teasing them.

As they laughed, Junie wondered how Mark would have reacted to the place. He probably would have embraced this project, planning a full-scale renovation in his mind.

She gestured to a quaint bay window. "Imagine a cozy breakfast nook right there."

April nodded approvingly. "You could plant herbs just outside the door, so they'd be in easy reach."

Junie loved that idea. "Fresh basil and rosemary would be nice."

At once, she was mentally filling the space with her kitchen things. She imagined cooking and entertaining her family and new friends here.

Could she do this? Her excitement was still tempered with doubt.

"You look like you're planning a cooking show of your own," Jo teased, snapping her back to reality.

Junie smiled. "Or a show about a thirty-something

woman who doesn't know the first thing about living alone or fixing up a house." She swung around to her mother. "Am I taking on more than I can handle? Be honest, Mom. Should I put in an offer or walk away?"

"You'll learn how to care for your home, sweetie," April reassured her. "Besides, you have all of us, including Deb. She'd love to help you decorate."

Jo winked. "If you mess up, I'm nearby. I can rally my friends on Sunshine Avenue to help. Especially with the garden. Everyone misses Mrs. Ashbury's citrus harvests. She used to give away bushels of it."

"You would have an orchard?" April asked. "I'd like to see that."

"This way," Junie said, leading her outside. "All of this goes with the house."

Standing at the edge of the lot, April shook her head. "This is a daunting project. It has been so neglected. Still, once you tend to it, it could be spectacular."

"Like Nana's garden." Junie smiled as she surveyed the weed-infested yard.

The idea appealed to her. She could work out her heartaches and frustrations in the garden. "I can't wait to get my hands dirty."

"Perhaps Maileah could help you until she finds work," April said.

"Maybe," Junie said. She often wished she were closer to Maileah, but her sister could be such a brat.

The thought of living alone for the first time was both intimidating and exhilarating to her. Mark's presence seemed to brush against her like a whisper.

Go for it.

Junie shivered. "You've seen it all, Mom. What do you think?"

April, perhaps sensing her hesitation, put her arm around Junie. "This house has good bones, and you have the money to make repairs. The location seems ideal. Plus, you'll have friends here and family nearby. And your job at the Majestic is a short walk or bike ride. I can see you living here."

Junie smiled, bolstered by her mother's confidence. "Nana recommended a real estate agent who can write an offer for me."

"That's probably her friend, Lauren."

"That's right," Junie said.

Shifting on her feet, Jo looked a little nervous. "Not that I'm trying to push you, but I don't think you should wait too long." She held up the key. "Want to lock your front door before we go?"

"Sure." Junie took the key and held it for a moment, feeling the enormity of what it meant. Jo and April walked ahead of her.

As Junie locked the door, leaving the quiet potential of the empty house, she hoped she was making the right decision. Yet, the promise of a different future buoyed her spirits. A tiny seed of excitement sprouted within her.

With a stirring sense of purpose, she put her hand on the door. As the lock clicked into place, she whispered, "I think you would have loved it here, Mark. I'll make you proud of me."

The air around her felt heavy with choices to be made. Which should she start on? The exterior in need of paint or a garden gasping for renewed life? Still, a newfound resolve bloomed in Junie. She could turn this property into a nest of her own.

With a shaking hand, she brought out her phone and dialed the person Nana had recommended. This was the first step toward reclaiming her life.

The phone rang, and Junie spoke to her. Lauren suggested she come by her office in an hour. "I'll see you soon," she said before hanging up.

Junie beamed and hurried to her mother and Jo, who were standing at the curb, peering at the house and others around it. "I'm so excited. Lauren can draw up the offer this afternoon."

"Why, that's wonderful, sweetheart." April hugged her. "Do you want me to go with you?"

"Would you? It's a big step...by myself." She didn't have to say anything; her mother knew she was thinking about Mark.

Junie handed the key to Jo. "I hope I'll be calling you my neighbor soon."

"I hope so, too," Jo said. "We have such fun here. We can even see the fireworks over the beach from here, although it's more fun to walk over there to watch them."

"Are you going to the Beach Festival this weekend?"

"Sure," Jo replied. "Want to come with me?"

April cast a look at Junie and smiled.

Jo caught that. "Oh, my gosh, Junie. Do you have a date?"

"I'm not sure." Junie felt a little self-conscious. "A couple of people have asked me, and I need to decide."

"Well, look at you go." Jo's eyes flashed with curiosity. "Now you have to tell me who."

Junie's cheeks warmed. "For one, Sailor."

Jo nodded in approval. "Nice guy. Knows how to fix anything and loves to travel. Who else?"

"Officer Blue." Recalling how nervous he had been, Junie almost felt like she was betraying his trust. But Jo was her friend.

However, Jo's reaction wasn't what Junie had thought it would be. "Blue?" she choked out.

"Do you know much about him?" Junie asked.

"I, uh… Yeah, he's a great guy. If he asked you…" Jo's voice trailed off, and she looked down, fidgeting with the key. "If he asked, then he must have meant it."

Junie sensed Jo was thinking about something else. "Is he seeing anyone else on Crown Island?"

"Nope. Not anymore." Jo jerked a thumb toward her car. "I'm needed at the diner. But hey, good luck with that."

"Thanks for letting me in the house again." Junie started to give her friend a hug, but Jo stepped back and trotted toward her car.

After Jo left, April turned to Junie. "That was a strange reaction. Do you think she might be interested in Blue?"

Junie passed a hand over her forehead. "You might be right. I think I stepped right in the middle of something." In that case, it would make her decision easier. "I should call Sailor. And let Blue know I can't make it."

As much as she liked Jo, she didn't want to get between her and Blue. She counted Jo as a friend. And hopefully, a new neighbor. Blue was nice enough, but she didn't feel any special attraction toward him.

As she thought about it, knowing that was a relief. Junie didn't want to force her feelings for anyone. It wouldn't be fair to the man, and she might grow to despise him because he simply wasn't Mark.

THAT AFTERNOON, Junie waited outside Whitley's office in the Majestic's executive suite. She had never been here, and it was different than she had imagined. It wasn't particularly plush, but it was comfortable. Sitting in a coral-colored wingback chair, she tried not to fidget.

Her nerves were already on edge after signing the offer on the house, although having her mother there helped. If the offer was accepted, that would be a huge step for her.

As for this pitch she was about to make, Junie had been considering it for some time, unlike the house. She'd practiced this bid for the gift shop space dozens of times.

I've owned a business before, and I can do it again. Of course, she'd had Mark then—her rock, her lover, her best friend. Having suffered through the grief of losing him, she was emerging from that dark space now. She felt stronger with him in her heart, where he would forever remain. She could talk to him anytime and often did, imagining his responses. What would he tell her now?

You go, girl.

She smiled to herself, feeling the warmth of the love that lingered in her heart. On her good days, Junie believed she wasn't completely alone. Other people might not understand that idea unless they've lost a spouse, a close friend, or a family member.

There weren't too many bad days for her now. Her mother had been right all along about finding a new purpose. And her father, she thought begrudgingly. When Junie had to rise and go to work, talk to people, and meet responsibilities, her mind was engaged, and that lessened the pain.

Even her sister Maileah helped with her recovery. If Junie counted her constant nagging.

The minute hand on the vintage clock in the waiting area ticked to the appointed hour, and the receptionist leaned back in her chair, glancing through Whitley's open door. "He's off the phone now," she said to Junie. "You can go in."

Drawing a deep breath for courage, she entered Whitley's office. A closet door stood ajar, and she spied a sea of colorful sports jackets.

Whitley rose as she walked in and clasped her hand. "Welcome, Junie. What brings you here today? The gift shop is running well, I trust." He tapped a printed spreadsheet on his desk. "Your financials look good. Sales are climbing." He gestured for her to sit.

"The new lines I've bought are performing well."

"And you're excellent with customers. We've received positive feedback from guests."

"I'm glad to hear that. I enjoy working with people and helping them find what they want. Surprise and delight, that's my approach. Customers should fall in love with what they're buying in my shop."

"You've certainly taken ownership of your position." He laced his hands on the desk and leaned forward, restating his initial question. "What can we do for you?"

"You just said I've taken ownership of the shop," Junie began. "I suppose that's only natural for me since I owned a business before. Part owner with my husband, that is. But I'm confident that I could manage this on my own."

Whitley listened, forcing her to continue. Junie forged ahead.

"While I appreciate the opportunity to manage the gift shop, I'm ready for a new challenge. I have a vision to not only expand the physical shop but also to take it online. And I believe that is outside of the scope of my current employment. Therefore, I have a proposal for you. For the Majestic Hotel, that is."

Whitley raised his brow, looking intrigued. "Go on."

Emboldened, Junie unpacked her ideas—bespoke souvenirs, curated local artistry, and an online storefront. With every point she made, she noticed Whitley's gaze becoming more thoughtful.

"You have a strong business sense, Junie," Whitley finally said. "Your vision aligns well with the quality the Majestic Hotel stands for."

Encouraged, Junie leaned in. "So, do you think it's feasible? To lease the space and run the gift shop independently?"

Whitley's eyebrows shot up. "You want to lease the space?"

Junie realized she'd left that part out. She'd been so excited with her plan. Feeling foolish now, she added, "Like Faye does with The Body Boutique. And the rest of the retailers in the hotel."

"The gift shop is different," Whitley said. "It's there to serve the guest needs, too."

Junie was aware of that, and she carried all the miniature toiletries people might need during their stay, from aspirins to shaving cream, although she was carrying better brands now.

"I would continue to offer those items as a service to

guests. But I want to expand merchandise offerings with my own branded products apart from the hotel's. If we agree that I will also offer convenience items for guests, then that space is no different from the others that are leased."

"I understand." Whitley's demeanor turned more serious. "Your plan has merit, Junie. And you have a valid argument. However, the hotel derives income from sales, and the conversion to a leased space is not my decision to make. I'm not sure how Mr. Ryan will perceive this. Leasing to an employee is uncharted territory."

"But I would no longer be an employee."

A lump formed in Junie's throat. She'd expected some hurdles, but then, hadn't she increased the income, making the shop more profitable?

"Could we at least present the proposal to him?" she asked.

Whitley met her eyes as if weighing her determination. "Of course, I'll bring it up with him, but I can't guarantee how he'll respond. He would have been more apt to consider it a few months ago before the shop became so profitable. With the renovation entering its costliest phase, we're having to balance the financials. I hope you'll understand. It's just business."

"Of course." Junie swallowed hard. "If that's the case..."

"Let me try," Whitley said. "We don't want to lose valuable assets to the hotel, either. You or the gift shop."

She appreciated his saying that, but she had to make sure he could convey her vision. "The Majestic might be changing, but significant growth often requires taking measured risks. I could make it so much more than it is."

Whitley listened, nodding.

"I know I can increase the revenue on Majestic Hotel-branded merchandise if I have more opportunity," Junie said. "Between a royalty and a lease payment, the Majestic would be about even with what it's earning now on the shop. And you wouldn't have to replace me. I know who was here before me."

She didn't mean that last comment as a dig, but it was the truth. The guy before had spent more time on his phone than helping customers.

Whitley nodded. "I'll see what I can do, but I don't want to get your hopes up."

Junie left the executive office suite with a mix of anticipation and trepidation. Convincing Ryan remained a significant obstacle, but at least she had pitched the idea.

For now, that sliver of possibility was enough to keep her motivated, fueled by the conviction that she was ready for this next chapter. As much as she liked working at the gift shop and the Majestic, she might have to leave to realize her dream.

She had some investments and enough to pay for the house, but leasing a new storefront and building up a business would require a lot more effort and cost, not to mention risk. The Majestic offered a built-in clientele. There was value in that. Whitley and Ryan knew that. And so did she.

Junie went downstairs to the gift shop and waved to Faye in the shop across the hall. "Thanks for watching it for me. Any customers while I was gone?"

"One man, but he said he'd come back," Faye said, tucking her short red curls behind one ear. "I was with someone. He said he's staying here." She glanced at a tall man who was walking toward them. "Oh, look. Here he is now." She wiggled her fingers at Junie and turned back to her shop.

Junie looked back and caught her breath. It was the attractive man she'd blasted into the other day. Embarrassment heated her cheeks.

6

*K*nox strolled into the gift shop of the Majestic Hotel, the door chiming softly as he entered. He paused to admire the vintage crystal chandelier overhead. The boutique-style space was thoughtfully curated, unlike most other hotel gift shops. It was more personal, more inviting—though it was slated for renovation as well. It didn't need much other than paint, but he spied an electrical cord with multiple items plugged in. Possibly an electrical upgrade, as Whitley had mentioned. He'd spent the morning with Ryan and his general manager.

He glanced around, his gaze landing on the woman behind the counter.

"Welcome," she said pleasantly. "May I help you find something?"

"I'll know it when I see it, but thanks." She had a nice voice and a pretty smile, he thought. Yet, something about her seemed familiar. She went back to work arranging a candle display.

Flicking a gaze in her direction, he took another look, admiring her long, sun-kissed hair, grace, and poise. If he were dating, she would be precisely his type.

He shook his head to dismiss the thought and redirected his attention toward his purpose. He had come here to find something to send to Penny, his daughter.

Knox browsed a small section devoted to creative wooden toys. He picked up a small wooden boat, inspecting the craftsmanship, which he appreciated. Penny loved playing on the beach. The toy seemed a nice souvenir for her—especially if he decided to take the job offer from Ryan and relocate to Crown Island.

The woman glanced up and caught his eye. "That's one of our bestsellers. Handmade by a local craftsman. It's more than just a toy; it's a piece of art. It comes apart, and children like to put it back together again. I'll show you." She joined him by the display.

Her voice had a warmth that matched her appearance, easing the web of decisions consuming him. If he took this position, he'd have to find a home quickly. To his surprise, his parents agreed to move with him so they could help care for Penny. They liked the prospect of mild winters after living in New Jersey.

Good for the old bones, his father had said. And for the injuries he'd sustained in his military service, although Doug MacKenzie rarely spoke of that.

Knox would have to act fast. Ryan needed someone to oversee the Majestic Hotel renovation right away, and Knox was eager to change positions before the beginning of first grade for Penny.

The woman in front of him shifted the wooden pieces with her tapered fingers. He was also acutely aware of her scent. She wore a light, fresh perfume that reminded him of flowers on a sunny beach.

"See, it's easy." She handed the piece back to him.

"My daughter would love this." His hand brushed hers as he took it, creating a fleeting connection, that to his surprise, he enjoyed.

"She's a lucky girl. How old is she?"

"She just turned six and will begin first grade in the fall."

"What a cute age," she said.

This woman had a brightness about her that rivaled the chandelier above. He couldn't help returning her magnetic smile. "I'll take it."

As he approached the counter to make the purchase, he felt her curious gaze on him. But now wasn't the time to start seeing anyone. His life was in flux, and the needs of his daughter came first.

The woman rang up the sale. "Would you like this gift-wrapped? I have children's gift bags."

"She'd like that." He watched her carefully wrap the item and slip it into a bright purple bag.

"That's her favorite color," Knox said.

"Mine, too, when I was a little girl." She tied a ribbon onto the bag. "Will you be staying long at the Majestic?"

"A few days." He hadn't made a firm decision, although he was close. "Do you like living on Crown Island?"

"I do," she said as she added a fluffy pink bow with rainbow streamers. "My grandmother and mother are from here. I just returned."

"What brought you back?"

She hesitated, and the smile slipped from her face. Immediately, he knew he'd touched on a sensitive topic.

"I'm only trying to understand the community. My name is Knox, by the way. I'm thinking of moving here."

"Junie. Nice to meet you." The smile returned to her lips. "Crown Island is easy going and very family friendly. Kids can play outside year-round. They ride bikes and go to the beach or the playground at the park. I think she'd like it." She applied a butterfly stick to the bag. "Have you driven around the neighborhoods?"

"I'm meeting a real estate agent in half an hour." He wanted to learn more about the area, and particularly the schools. Penny was a smart girl who needed to be challenged.

Junie beamed. "I just put an offer on a house. I think you'll find plenty of things for kids to do, along with nice restaurants and activities for you and your wife."

"I'm not married," Knox replied quickly. "And I don't date."

"I didn't ask," Junie said pointedly, followed by another quick smile of amusement. "Well, then. I hope your daughter enjoys this."

He tucked the bag under his arm. "I appreciate your help." He turned and walked toward the door, then stopped. Suddenly, he knew where he'd seen her. Turning around, he snapped his fingers. "We've met before. You were the woman in a hurry the other day."

Junie's face colored slightly. "Sorry about that." She wagged her phone. "You saved it, though. Thank you."

"Glad to be of service, Junie." He even liked the pleasant sound of her name.

He strode out, chastising himself for his comment. Why did he offer that information? He'd been using that excuse as a shield after Lola broke his heart and took off, but he should have seen that coming. He'd met her at a rock concert when they were younger. They dated a little, and when Lola became pregnant, he insisted on marrying her. His parents were shocked, but they were also thrilled to be grandparents.

Lola had taken off shortly after giving birth to Penelope, saying that motherhood wasn't for her after all.

But one look in his child's bright blue eyes was all it took for Knox to fall completely in love with the tiny baby he called Penny. He would never abandon her, even though his friends wondered how he would manage without Lola to care for her. Adoption had never crossed his mind until one of his New York friends mentioned it. Knox had been appalled. That had angered him so much that he'd vowed to make up for her mother's absence.

Penny would have the best life he could provide.

He wasn't cut out for the big city anyway. He and his folks had moved a lot with the military. He'd never thought he'd land here, but Ryan Kingston was the best boss he'd ever had. He'd encouraged Knox to keep Penny and gave him time off when she was ill.

The last he'd heard from Lola was when she sent him divorce papers. She was following a rock band on tour and couldn't be bothered to return, even to see her child.

Since Penny had never known her mother, she didn't miss her. Still, Knox and his parents showered the little girl with love to compensate for it.

He glanced back over his shoulder at Junie through the shop window. Something about her intrigued him. As if she felt his gaze on her, she looked up. He lifted his hand and turned away, his heart skipping.

. . .

"THERE IT IS," Knox said as the real estate agent slowed the car in front of a neat blue home with navy trim, white shutters, and a sign in front.

A kaleidoscope of colors spun into focus on the street they'd turned on, although that wasn't any different from other streets on the island. Everywhere he looked was a blaze of color. Penny would love it.

"A corner lot is always nice," Kellie said.

She was a real estate agent in her mid-forties and had lived on Crown Island all her life. Whitley had suggested her. Knox liked her because she had three children and knew all about the schools and teachers.

Kellie turned off the engine and got out of the car. "This house is fully renovated with a new kitchen and bathrooms, refinished hardwood floors, and custom shutters."

"That's a plus," Knox said. He started up the walkway.

Looking at the house, he was immediately struck by the similarity to one of the houses he'd grown up in. A wide wrap-around front porch, mature trees Penny could climb, and a corner lot with room in the back for jet skis when she got a little older. A swing already hung from one tree for her. He hardly needed to go into the house to know he liked it.

If his parents could find a house nearby, it would be perfect. This one had a thriving garden they would like. They were young retirees. His mother liked to stay active, and his father needed to. "Are there any other houses for sale on this street?"

Kellie looked doubtful. "There is one, but it's much smaller and quite rundown." She pointed to a sad-looking house with peeling paint.

"What about that vacant lot in between?" he asked.

"It goes with the other house, which is part of an estate sale. I've heard it's rough—inside and out. Shall we walk through this beauty?"

"Sure," Knox said.

The other house wouldn't suit his parents as it was, but it could be renovated to their liking. Or he could live in that one. Still, an extensive renovation could take a year. It might need new electrical, plumbing, and a roof before he even started on the interior.

If he were to accept Ryan's offer of project manager, he'd be busy enough at work and caring for Penny. He would have little time left over to manage another construction project.

When Knox stepped inside the ocean-blue house, he smiled and nodded. "As advertised."

It had gleaming wood floors, double-paned windows, and custom lighting—even more than was on his checklist.

"This one has two primary suites," Kellie said. "There's an extra room in the back that would suit your parents when they visit."

"That's a plus."

They walked through the kitchen, bedrooms, and bathrooms, all of which were to his liking. The kitchen had pearly white and gray marble countertops with tasteful white cabinetry. The blue-and-white beach-themed tiles on the backsplash would delight Penny. The bathrooms followed a similar theme.

"This will meet my needs perfectly," Knox said.

Kellie's face brightened. "Does that mean you'd like me to write an offer?"

Knox stared out the kitchen window at the overgrown lot and the tired house on the other side. It was an eyesore, and he could only imagine the creatures scurrying around. Probably rats.

However, there was one way to improve the neighborhood and make it safe for Penny.

His parents could live in the second suite while the other house was under renovation. He could hire a contractor, and that would give his parents something to do. They could design and outfit the house to their liking. And they would love to bring the overgrown garden back to life.

Knox nodded to himself at his idea; it was a good one. He turned to Kellie. "Make an offer on this house, and on the one next door."

This was perfect, and he could hardly wait to surprise his parents.

7

*M*aileah stared at the wedding invitation and pressed the phone to her ear, a mix of disbelief and anger swirling within her. "Hawk will be at the wedding?"

Her ex-boyfriend's name left a sour taste in her mouth. She flopped back onto her bed, wondering why she'd even bothered to answer her father's phone call. He might be her father, but she was the one still panting after him like a puppy looking for an approving pat on the head.

"Of course, he's invited," her father responded, his voice displaying a level of nonchalance that further inflamed her. "Hawk has been a good friend to Olga. We all had such fun dancing. You were having a good time, too."

Maileah tried to block those memories. Olga—the woman who stole her father away from her mother. She also had the dubious distinction of having slept with Maileah's boyfriend.

"Let me get this straight," she said. "You're inviting the

man who had a fling with your fiancé and who was dating your daughter at the same time?" Her voice wavered as painful memories ripped through her mind.

"We've moved past that," her father replied, dismissively. "Olga is young. A bit of recklessness is to be expected."

"This is too bizarre, even for you, Dad." Maileah clenched her jaw and tried to breathe without screaming. "So, you're saying it's alright for Olga to act the same way you did with Mom?"

"I always had deep respect for your mother." Her father responded in that professorial way he had that drove Maileah to the edge.

"I'm confused," she said. "You thought your *respect* for her excused your countless indiscretions?" Her voice trembled with a mixture of fury and pain.

"You're young and immature. Once you experience a committed, long-term relationship, you'll understand the complexities," her father said, droning on in his calculated, controlling way. "A marriage survives because of compromise. Your mother used to be good at that. Understanding, even."

"Oh, I understand," she shot back. "I broke it off with Hawk the first time he cheated on me, because a cheater always repeats his actions. Isn't that right, Dad? In your professional opinion, that is."

"May, you need to grasp the realities of life. The world isn't as black and white as you or your mother think it is. If she had considered my feelings, she would have agreed that I was merely following the course of nature. I am still a virile man whose responsibility is to—"

"Stop it," Maileah said, cutting him off. "I am not

falling for your psycho mumble jumble anymore. And my name is Maileah now," she said coldly. "I've had it legally changed. And your kind of *reality*? I want no part of it."

"May, you're my only contact with the family," Calvin went on, ignoring everything she'd said. "You and I have a special relationship. Your mother and Junie are wallowing in self-pity. They are under the mistaken impression that I did them harm. In reality, I acted in a logical manner, and they fell victim to societal expectations that warped their perception."

"Seriously, what do you want?" It was all Maileah could do to keep from slamming the phone against the wall. Why did she think he would ever change?

"Olga would like you to be her maid of honor," Calvin replied. "She has even chosen a dress for you." He named a bargain discount store. "It's on sale, so it's well within your budget. That was very thoughtful of her."

"Be in the wedding?" Maileah squeaked in disbelief. "There's no way I can do that."

Calvin cleared his throat. "I can lend you money if you need it. Since you're an adult, Olga and I have decided that you are to stand on your own now. It would be wrong for you to expect us to pay for your expenses, don't you agree?"

He had missed the entire point. Maileah sighed. "Especially given the cost of her fancy shoes and designer wedding dress I saw in her posts all over social media." She'd had the empire style altered to fit during her pregnancy. "Wasn't that a Givenchy?"

"Valentino," Calvin said, correcting her.

How could such an intelligent man be so dense? Maileah slapped her forehead. "Who do you think you are? And how are you paying for all this?"

Her father sighed, a weary release into a widening chasm. "Will you join us on this happy occasion?"

"Absolutely not."

"Do you plan to hold this grudge until the baby is born?"

"What do you think?" She hung up, not waiting for another of his long-winded, self-centered answers. He could twist reality inside out, and she'd finally had enough. Maileah suspected Olga had lied about her pregnancy to get Calvin to marry her. But she was pregnant now. Whether it was Calvin's or Hawk's baby, who could tell? As far as Maileah was concerned, they all deserved each other.

The revelation of her father's acceptance of Olga's actions and his expectation of Maileah's acceptance was simply too much.

What her father saw in that woman, Maileah couldn't say, especially to her mother. He even had the nerve to insist that Maileah call him Calvin when they were out clubbing with Olga and Hawk. Her father was so hung up on his age. He'd had a facelift and a hair transplant when Olga teased him about looking so much older than she was.

Maileah snorted and tossed the invitation into the trash. Junie had already burned her invitation over the kitchen sink. Her sister was the smart one. She bit her lip, trying to hold back the angry tears that spilled onto her cheeks, but the hurt and disillusionment were too great.

A soft tap sounded on the door.

"Hey, are you okay?"

It was Junie.

Maileah's first thought was to tell her to go away, but she felt so lonely and adrift. Sniffing, she rolled from the bed and opened the door.

"Was that Dad?" Junie asked.

Maileah could only nod. When Junie took her in her arms, she broke down, sobbing onto her shoulder. "Oh, Junie, why is he so awful? Why can't we have a nice, boring father like everyone else?"

Junie ran her hand over Maileah's hair. "I don't know, but I wish we did. You don't have to talk to him, you know. I'm not."

"That's why he keeps calling me," Maileah said. "Supposedly, Olga wants me to be in the wedding. Can you imagine what that would do to Mom? She's been through enough. I don't know if Dad was always like that, and she shielded us, or if he's gotten worse."

"Both, I think," Junie said.

Maileah flopped onto the bed, and Junie sat cross-legged beside her. Not only was Maileah distraught over that phone call, but she was also feeling guilty about how she had treated her sister.

She drew a sleeve across her damp eyes. "Look at us. We've traded places. When you were suffering, I was the one who had it all together, or I thought I did. I know I wasn't very nice to you, but it hurt me to see you so depressed after Mark died. And now, I'm the mess, and you're off working and buying a house."

Junie smoothed a hand over Maileah's tangled hair. "We all go through ups and downs. This is only temporary. You'll probably be back on top soon." She hesitated. "You're not thinking of going to the wedding, are you?"

"No way. Hawk will be there, too. I wish I could wipe all that from my past. I'm so ashamed now. At first, Olga seemed like a lot of fun. Dad acted like we had a delicious secret and made it seem so cool and sophisticated. He told me that he and Mom had an open marriage."

"Only on his side," Junie said, curling her lip in disgust.

"I never told Mom that." Maileah felt like her world was crashing down around her, and worse, she was partly to blame. "What if I had told him what he was doing was wrong? That I didn't want to have anything to do with him, Olga, or his mid-life crisis? Maybe I could have stopped the divorce. Instead, I put a bow on it."

"No, you didn't," Junie said. "We're not to blame for what he did. Not you, not Mom, not me. Dad twists words and tries to make us think that way."

"Is he what you'd call a narcissist or a psychopath?" Maileah asked.

Junie shook her head. "I don't know, but he sure seems to fit the descriptions he teaches. I wonder if he recognizes that."

Maileah reached for her. "I'm such a wreck, and I'm so sorry for all the things I said to you."

"Thank you for saying that," Junie said softly, taking her hand. "Get some rest, and like you used to tell me, get up and get out. You'll feel better if you do."

"I'll try." Maileah had to find work soon. She loved her mother and grandmother, but she had lived on her own for so many years. She missed her privacy, and she didn't want to burden them.

Junie hugged her again. "And don't answer when Dad calls. If it's an emergency, someone else will reach us."

Maileah nodded. "When did my baby sister get so smart?"

Junie gave her a small smile. "We'll see about that."

Her sister's tone sounded different. "Why? What's up?"

"I'm worried that my offer on the house might not be accepted. Even though it's rough, the heirs are willing to take a lot less than it's worth for a quick cash sale. But it's perfect for me. I'd love to fix it up."

"I could help," Maileah said quickly. Another thought crossed her mind, but she thought better of asking Junie about it. She would wait to see if her sister got the house.

Junie nudged her. "Hey, Sailor asked if we'd like to take surfing lessons. You should come with me."

"I couldn't."

"Come on. You'd be doing me a favor." Junie grinned. "My sister used to tell me to get out there, and I don't want to let her down."

"Who is Sailor?"

"He runs the bike concession at the Majestic Hotel. He's also a champion surfer."

"Really?" Maileah sat up.

"Sailor travels some, and one of his cousins takes over for him when he's gone." Junie paused, thinking about his invitation. She really liked Sailor, but she wanted to learn more about him.

"Are you interested in him?"

"Maybe. Sailor is easygoing, and a lot of girls like him. He's easy on the eyes, for sure." Junie felt odd saying that. "He invited me out this weekend, but I haven't accepted yet. The idea of dating still feels strange. Like I'm betraying Mark. No one else has given me the feeling I had with him." Even as she spoke, she couldn't help thinking about the guy she'd run into at the hotel. That encounter had been a little disturbing.

"Junie, it's been two years."

"I know." She shrugged that off. "Anyway, Mom knows

Sailor's dad, Adrian, who owns Regal Bikes in town. He also jams on the guitar at Cuppa Jo's on Friday nights. You should come. That's where I meet a lot of people in town. And at the Majestic, of course."

Maileah scrubbed her face with her palms. "Sounds like you've created a life here. I'm sorry I said what I did about the gift shop being beneath you. If you're satisfied there, then I guess it's okay. It's not like you have to work. Not like I do."

"I like it well enough for now," Junie said, ignoring the hint of jealousy. Still, she liked the thrill of building a larger business, just to see if she could. She loved sharing unique finds that surprised and delighted people. But she wasn't quite ready to share that with Maileah yet.

"We haven't always gotten along, and a lot of that has been my fault," Maileah said.

Junie bumped against her. "Let's work on that."

"I'll try not to pick fights," Maileah said, dipping her chin. "Sometimes I wonder why I do that."

Junie put her arm around her sister. "Come learn to surf with me. The waves and fresh air will do you good." Junie wasn't sure if they'd ever be as close as their mother and her friend Deb were, but they could try.

8

*A*fter dinner with their mother and grandmother, Junie shared the dishwashing and drying with her sister. As she finished the last of the dishes, she peered from the kitchen window.

"Looks like a full moon out tonight. The waves should be great." She bumped her sister's hip. "Want to walk on the beach?"

"I don't know," Maileah said.

Something was bothering Maileah, Junie could tell. "Well, I do. It will do you good. Isn't that what you used to tell me?"

"If I hear you say that one more time…"

"Let's go." Junie popped her with a dishtowel.

"Hey, stop that."

"Make me," Junie said, laughing.

Suddenly, they reverted to childhood, and Junie dashed for the door with Maileah in pursuit.

"Going to the beach," Junie called out to their mother

and grandmother, who were sitting on the back porch with the doors and windows open.

"Race you," Maileah said, edging her out of the doorway.

They ran down Beach View Lane and across the street to the beach. Vigorous waves brought on by the high tide crashed onto the shore under the vast, moonlit sky. The balmy air held magical energy that Junie loved, yet few people were out tonight.

"You always were a brat," Maileah said, puffing as they hit the sand.

Catching her breath, Junie grinned. "At least I grew out of it."

"That's because you were Mom's favorite. I got stuck with Dad, so I never had a chance."

Junie turned to Maileah, exasperated. "You're always complaining about Mom, but she's the one who has held our family together."

"Yeah, and she never lets us forget it."

As the ocean breeze whipped around her, Junie caught her hair and twisted it into a makeshift knot. "What are you really upset about?"

Maileah twisted her mouth to one side and let out a small puff of air. "You actually want to know?"

"I'm asking, aren't I?"

Her sister waved her arms. "You were always the adored one. Oh, look at her walking. Look at her, a big first grader. Oh, what a beautiful bride."

Junie put her hands on her hips. "That's it, isn't it? My wedding." The rest of what Maileah said was kid stuff. Literally.

Maileah shrugged and faced out to sea. "It should have been me first."

"Marrying Blake would have been a disaster, and you know it." Junie stopped. "He's already on divorce number two."

"Maybe they weren't the right ones for him. Maybe I was." She charged off again.

Junie trotted to keep up. "I told you what I saw. And I wasn't the only one."

When Maileah was hoping for a proposal around the time of Junie's wedding, her boyfriend was secretly seeing another woman. Junie and Mark had slipped away from the reception for a break when they saw Blake with her in a dark alcove.

"But I really wanted him, Junie. If you hadn't told me, Blake and I might still be together."

"He was cheating on you." Junie still recalled the cloud that had descended on her wedding day. How could she not have warned her sister?

"Guys make mistakes."

Junie shook her head. "That sounds like a line some guy has given you." When color rose in Maileah's cheeks as confirmation, she knew she'd nailed it. "He did this at your sister's wedding with the whole family around. It was like he wanted to get caught, don't you see?"

Maileah averted her gaze.

"Wanting something desperately doesn't make it so," Junie said. "Marriage is a lot more than that. Trust me, you're better off without him."

"So what if we divorced?" Maileah kicked a rushing wave, sending a splash across Junie's jeans. "At least I would have been married and maybe had a couple of kids. I'm so tired of people asking me why I'm not married. And believe it or not, I really would have liked to have children."

Seeing the pained look in her sister's eyes, Junie stopped and took her hand. "That I understand," she said softly.

Maileah's expression crumpled. "I shouldn't have said that."

"I'm glad you did. People can't help you unless you let them in." She touched Maileah's flushed cheek. "Try not to let it bother you when some insensitive clod asks why you're not married." She gave her sister a wry grin. "When they ask me, my answer always puts them in their place."

"Can I borrow that excuse?"

She squeezed Maileah's hand, and they continued walking, dodging the waves. "You don't want it. And you don't set out to be a divorced mother of two. Being a mother seems hard enough with a partner. I'd rather be a single mother than married to a man who abused me—mentally or physically."

"Some women get stuck, though."

"And many get unstuck. Look at what Mom has been through. What if we'd been younger? Imagine how hard that would have been on her."

Maileah made a face. "Do you think she told us everything Dad has done?"

"What do you think?"

"That she kept a lot from us. Maybe we're the reason she stayed."

"She tried to keep the family together," Junie said, stooping to pick up an interesting shell.

Maileah heaved a sigh. "That makes me feel sad...and a little guilty. If not for us, she could have left him earlier."

"Mom wanted children." Junie paused, turning over the

shell before tossing it back into the sea. "None of us can foresee the future. We make the best decisions we can at the time. Who cares what anyone else thinks? That's what she told me when Mark died."

"And why you never wore black?" Maileah asked. "That is, when you managed to get out of your pajamas or his old shirts."

Junie gave a sister a small smile. "Mark had such a big, happy soul. I couldn't bear to think of him as ceasing to exist or of honoring him in anything but his favorite outfit at his funeral. I could feel his presence around me, and he always liked me in bright colors. Even though I was destroyed, I felt he never left me. How could I not wear his favorite yellow dress?"

Maileah hugged her. "That's why my younger sister is my role model."

"Still, I'm worried about Mom and what she's going to do. Death is final, but divorce…"

"Yeah. That jerk is still our dad."

Junie paused. "Think of how much farther ahead Mom would have been in her career without him. You know, she did a lot of his work. All that research and the articles she wrote for him. And a lot more."

Maileah twisted her lips to one side. "When I was little, I used to think she was the professor. And I thought he ran the university."

Junie raised her brow at that. "Patriarch-ing much?"

Heaving another sigh, Maileah shook her head. "With Dad as my role model, maybe that's why I was attracted to Blake and Hawk and all those other guys that treated me like dirt."

Junie hadn't made that connection, but Maileah had a

point. "I'm not a therapist, but you might want to talk to one about that."

"It's as if the worse they are, the more I want their attention. When I get it, I feel like I've won something." Maileah lingered, tracing the sand with the toe of her sneaker. "Do you remember how we'd go out as a family, and Dad was always checking out other women in front of Mom? I stopped bringing friends home because he creeped them out."

"I remember all of that. I did the same."

"We were teenagers—not even old enough to drive. We shouldn't have even been aware of stuff like that." Tentatively, Maileah reached for Junie. "I understand why you didn't want me to go through that with Blake. You were looking out for me—even though it ruined your wedding."

"It didn't, and you were not the one at fault," Junie said. "I'd had my share of lousy boyfriends when Mark came along. He opened my eyes to what a good man was. I wanted that for you, too."

Maileah embraced her. "How do I find that?"

"Give the nice guys a chance."

"Don't you think they're kind of dull?"

Junie's heart thumped at the memory of her husband. "Mark was anything but that."

"How do you know when you find the right one?" Maileah asked.

"It's hard to explain, but I felt it when I met him." Junie stood, looking out to sea. How could she explain this to her sister? She'd had a visceral reaction the first time she'd met Mark, as if he was giving off electromagnetic signals. They had even talked about it, and he'd felt the same vibe when they met.

"What was different about him?" Maileah asked.

"The only way I can describe the feeling is that when I was dating other guys, I would wonder if they were *the one*. The right fit for me. But when I met Mark, I didn't even think about it. I just knew."

"That's not much help," Maileah said, turning back toward the house.

Junie followed, brushing mist from her face. "Just trust yourself. If you have to ask that question, then also ask yourself why you're wondering. Maybe there's something about him you find irritating, and you're squashing that feeling. But it counts."

Maileah nodded. "Like when he checks out other women in your presence. I wonder if Dad did that when he and Mom were dating."

"I don't know, but that's a serious red flag."

"You know, Hawk did that with Olga," Maileah said, looking thoughtful. "I ignored it because she dressed for attention, and guys were always checking her out."

Junie touched her sister's hand. "See? You felt it. You knew something was wrong. Listen to your instincts."

"Thanks," Maileah said. "This helps a lot."

"I like it when we're not snarky with each other," Junie said.

"Me, too." Maileah poked her in the side. "But what if that's my normal way of relating to you? You must admit some of it is kind of fun. You're still my kid sister."

Junie laughed. "If you weren't like that at all, I'd know something was seriously wrong with you."

As they headed home, Junie wondered if she would ever find that feeling she'd had with Mark again. Despite the advice she'd just given to her sister, she questioned her ability to compromise to have the family she so desperately wanted.

Would she end up in a marriage like their mother had? Junie tipped her head back, searching the starlit canopy for an answer, but there was no sign to guide her. Even though she often felt Mark's presence, she really was on her own.

9

*J*unie slid onto a red vinyl stool at Cuppa Jo's. She wasn't there to eat, even though she was on her lunch break. When she called out to Jo, her friend turned around.

"Got a minute?" Junie had come at a slow time on purpose. She needed to mend the chilly situation with Jo, especially if the offer on the house across the street from her was accepted.

"Okay." Jo motioned to another woman behind the counter that she was taking a break. "Let's take that booth."

Junie followed her across the black-and-white tiled floor. The vintage diner had become her local hangout, and she'd been coming to the Friday night local jam sessions. She often sat with Blue and his friends, but she hadn't thought anything about it until he asked her out.

After they sat down, Jo laced her fingers on the tabletop. "You're probably wondering why I've been acting so weird."

"I thought it might be about Blue," Junie said, taking a chance.

"Maybe you didn't know that we used to date." Jo twiddled her fingers with nervous energy.

"I didn't. And I never thought of Blue as anything but a friend." That was the truth; she'd been surprised when he asked her out.

"If you really like him, you should go out with him," Jo said. "He's a good guy."

Junie sensed that her friend was holding something back. "My grandmother once said that Blue was complicated. After what I've been through with my husband, I don't want to make any mistakes."

Jo nodded thoughtfully. "Ella was probably referring to Blue's brother. They served on the police force together in Chicago, and when Charles was killed in the line of duty, it nearly destroyed Blue. He quit and left the city. It took him a long time to recover from the tragedy. He still has nightmares about it. But that's how he landed on Crown Island. He was looking for a small town, and the community was lucky to have him with his experience."

Junie touched Jo's hand. "Do you still care for him?"

"I shouldn't." Jo shrugged. "I told him I wasn't ready to make a commitment."

Junie wondered about that. She'd also seen how Blue seemed to brighten in Jo's presence. "He still comes to the diner, though."

"And it's hard to see him talking to other women," Jo said. "It's my problem, I know. I'm the one who let him go. But you should go out with him. I know he's lonely. I was only surprised, that's all."

Junie watched her friend, whose body language didn't

match her words. She took Jo's hands in hers. "Blue seems like a great guy, but he's not for me. As I think about it, he didn't really want to ask me out. He was awfully nervous, like he was forcing himself. When I told him I had to think about it, he seemed relieved."

Jo raised her eyes. "Really?"

Junie nodded. "I was fortunate to have a wonderful marriage. That's why it's been so tough to get over Mark's death. I know what real love feels like. That compelling, irresistible feeling of connecting with someone. There's a reason people use the term *soulmates*." She paused and squeezed Jo's hands. "Blue is a terrific guy, but he'll never be my soulmate, and I'll never be his."

Tears welled in Jo's eyes, and she nodded. "You know how it feels then. I was so excited to have you move in across the street, but when you mentioned Blue, I fell apart. If the two of you were together, that would rip my heart out every day. Still, if you were the one for him, I'd have to somehow be happy for him. Especially since I was the one who tossed him back."

"I think he still cares for you. If he didn't, he wouldn't come to Cuppa Jo's."

"That's been hard," Jo said. "But I didn't have the heart to throw him out, either. It's a small town, so what are you going to do? I wish we could turn back time. I was scared because my parent's divorce was so acrimonious. I never want to go there."

"Maybe you and Blue are both afraid to try again."

Jo wiped a tear that trickled onto her cheek. "He wouldn't believe me if I said I was ready now. I love him, but how do I tell him I didn't mean what I said? The truth is one of his bedrock beliefs."

Suddenly, Junie had an idea. "Will you trust me?"

Jo blew out a breath. "What have I got to lose?"

"Be ready to go to the fireworks this weekend." Junie decided she would accept Blue's invitation.

Sailor's, too. He was cute and appealing, but not in a heart-pounding way like Mark. Still, her grandmother's words floated into her mind. She supposed she should at least try out a date or two.

They talked a little more, and Jo asked if she'd heard anything about her offer on the house.

"Not yet, but I'm hoping to hear good news soon." Just thinking about this big step filled her with a mixture of trepidation and excitement, though the latter feeling was surging ahead.

"Several people are talking about it," Jo said, drawing her brow. "Right before you came in, I overheard another agent talking about it with a client."

"Are they still here?" Junie twisted in her seat, searching the dining area.

"They left before you arrived."

A sense of foreboding filled Junie, and she tapped the table in thought. "I think I'll drive by again on the way back to work."

After leaving Cuppa Jo's, Junie steered her golf cart toward Sunshine Avenue. It was on the way to the Majestic anyway.

She slowed the cart as she approached and pulled to the curb across the street. Seeing her house with clearer eyes now, she realized the extent of work it needed. But she had the money to renovate it. The house needed saving, and so did she.

A movement near the house caught her attention, and

she leaned forward to get a better look. When she saw who it was, her chest tightened. It was the guy she'd seen in her shop. *Knox.* What on earth was he doing here?

He was walking around the exterior of the house. *Her house.* Suddenly, her senses went on high alert. He'd told her he was looking at homes to buy. She held her breath. Did he know this house was available?

Knox cut in front of the vacant lot and headed toward the other house for sale. She breathed out a sigh of relief. That nice one was more his style. But there were so many other houses on the island for sale, too. The chance that he'd buy anything on this street was slim.

Watching him, she couldn't help admiring his powerful, measured gait. His wavy, dark auburn hair was brushed back, reminding her of the Scottish hero in the television series she'd been binging on. This was a man who knew his worth. She blew out a breath.

Just then, her phone buzzed in her pocket, and she scrambled to pull it out. It was Lauren, her agent.

Junie answered. "Please tell me it's good news."

"I wish I could," Lauren replied. "Your offer came in first, and it was looking good. However, I have it on good authority that another agent called the estate attorney, too. It seems another offer is on its way, and the sellers want to look at that one as well. I know that's not the way it should be done, and I apologize for that."

Junie's hopes plummeted. "Do you know when they might have an answer?"

"Tomorrow, I hope. And I'll continue looking for other houses you might like."

"But I love this location, and Jo is just across the street." Junie narrowed her eyes. Was Knox responsible for the competitive bid? She watched him pause by the overgrown garden. "Should I increase my offer?"

"You could," Lauren replied. "But I know you'll get extra consideration with your cash offer. I'll try to find out, although I doubt the attorney handling the estate will tell me anything. However, maybe I can get a feel for which way the sellers might go."

Junie hadn't been thinking of buying a house when Jo mentioned this one, but now that she'd made an offer, she was emotionally invested.

If she wasn't meant to have this house, she would accept that and move on, but she liked the idea of having a friend across the street. Living alone was a huge step for her. Even though her family lived nearby, she feared she'd be lonely rattling around any place by herself. The picture that Jo had painted of a friendly neighborhood appealed to her.

With Maileah staying at their grandmother's house and her mother sleeping on a pull-out sofa, Junie felt like she should move out now to give them more space. Her sister had nowhere else to go, and neither did her mother.

She could offer them a guest room here, she thought. Once it was habitable.

Junie watched Knox as she spoke to Lauren. He was circling the updated house on the corner now. "I will increase the offer if needed. Let me know."

"I will. But try not to get too attached to the house. Often, when you lose out on a house, a better one surfaces."

Junie doubted that, however, Lauren assured her she would keep in close contact.

When Junie hung up, she noticed Knox walking toward her.

"Hey," he called out. "I'm surprised to see you here."

She steeled herself against his friendly demeanor. "It's a small island. What brings you this way?"

Knox smiled. "I'm making an offer on those two houses. I think my daughter will be excited."

Junie nodded, trying not to give anything away. "There are a lot of nice houses on Crown Island."

"This is a great neighborhood; I've got a good feeling about this. Do you live around here?" He held her gaze with a hopeful expression.

"Not too far," Junie replied, trying not to be taken in by his affable nature.

She wondered how many women had fallen in love with that dark ginger hair and even darker lashes that framed incredible eyes.

She averted her gaze. "My friend lives on this street."

That was close enough to the truth.

Knox took a step closer. "Maybe you could introduce me. I don't know anyone on Crown Island except my boss." He gestured toward the vacant lot. "My parents agreed to move with me if I take this position. I'd bet they could bring that garden back to life in one season."

Knox's enthusiasm was evident, and she wanted to be happy for him, but not for this property. She'd seen it first. "Have you accepted the job offer?"

"I decided five minutes ago," he said, grinning. "My agent dropped me off. She is delivering the offer, but I wanted to walk the property again."

Not knowing what to say, Junie merely nodded, but her stomach flopped as her spirits sank.

"Everything is coming together," Knox continued blithely. "The job, the house, a place for my parents. That other house needs a lot of work, but it shouldn't take too long."

"I don't know. Looks pretty sad to me." Junie didn't like withholding information from him, but he was now her rival. "Surely you could find something in better shape."

"The location is perfect. We'd both have our privacy, and they can help look after Penny."

Junie bit her lip, squelching her desire to lash out. "Well, good luck to you. I must go back to work now."

Knox looked over his shoulder. "If it's not too much trouble, could you give me a lift to the Majestic? I was going to walk back to get a feel for the neighborhood."

"That's a good idea," Junie said, seizing on that.

"But you can probably tell me just as much."

No question, Knox was intriguing, and the way he seemed to look right into her made her shiver. Feeing conflicted, Junie sighed.

"Get in." How long could it take? Surely she could contain herself that long.

Knox slid onto the bench seat beside her, and Junie started the golf cart. His thigh brushed against hers. She gulped and shifted. Just then, her phone buzzed. She glanced at it.

It was Lauren.

"Do you need to get that?" he asked.

She didn't want to tip her hand to Knox, and the Majestic was only five minutes away. Her heart quickened with tension. "It can wait."

Junie pressed the pedal, willing the old golf cart on, though its top speed wasn't very fast. As she approached the main thoroughfare of Orange Avenue, Knox's phone rang.

He glanced at it. "It's my real estate agent," he said, smiling. "Hello?"

Worried, Junie pumped the pedal. Surely this old cart had a little extra speed in it.

"Another offer?" Knox said into the phone. "Well, increase my bid. I want that property."

Junie could barely make out the other person's words. *By how much?* She jerked the steering wheel, cutting off another cart, and as she did, Knox slid across the seat.

"Hang on," she said.

Knox bobbled his phone, but this time, he wasn't quick enough, and his phone sailed from his grip. "Hey," he cried. "What are you trying to do? Stop. I need to find my phone."

"Oh, my gosh, I'm sorry." She pulled to the curb, feeling slightly guilty. "Did you see where it went?"

Knox gave her an exasperated look. "That was an important call."

"The wheel slipped," she said nonchalantly, her guilt escalating. "I haven't driven this finicky old cart in a while. It's my grandmother's. Need me to wait for you?"

"If it's not too much trouble," he said, his voice dripping with sarcasm. He stepped from the cart and strode onto the corner property. He paced the area, mumbling to himself.

Junie couldn't stand it. She needed to drop him off before she returned Lauren's call, but she couldn't exactly leave him. Or could she?

"If that's going to take a while," she began, drumming her fingers on the wheel.

"I could use a little help," he said. "If you hadn't been driving like a maniac, we wouldn't be here."

Junie rolled her eyes. *What a jerk.* Just when she was beginning to like him. Up until he decided to go after her house, that is. "I really must get back. The Majestic isn't that far."

Knox put his hands on his hips. "Are you serious?"

"Oh, all right. I'm coming." Junie stretched one foot toward the pavement.

He held up a hand. "On second thought, don't bother." He stopped beside a flower planter. After parting the flowers, he pulled out his phone. "Got it. I'll walk the rest of the way."

"Come on. I'm sorry," Junie said. She patted the seat beside her.

Knox tapped his phone, mumbling under his breath again. "It's not working. Now I'll have to get my phone fixed. Or buy a new one. I don't need your kind of *help* anymore. Go on." He waved her off.

"If you insist," Junie retorted, incensed at his reaction. "You should hang on next time."

"Well, you should learn how to drive," he shot back, his face darkening.

"Oh, yeah?" What a privileged idiot, she thought. "I drive just fine. It's not my fault life throws curves."

"Wait a minute," he said, advancing toward her. "You were sitting in front of that house. Are you the one who made an offer on it?"

Trembling with anger, Junie didn't answer. She started the cart and took off, her competitive nature taking over.

In less than two minutes, she could make that call. Junie didn't dare slow down now. In her rearview mirror, she could see Knox trotting behind her.

She knew what he was up to. He planned to call from

the hotel and raise his offer. She pressed the pedal again, trying to lose him in their slow-motion race toward the finish line.

As she careened over a speed bump into the employee parking entrance, she saw her friend Faye wave at her.

"Can't stop," Junie called out, nearly bouncing from her seat.

Faye jumped aside. "Gee, slow down, Junie."

"I have an emergency." Junie parked and sprinted from the cart, pulling out her phone. From the corner of her eye, she saw Knox racing across the lawn to the front entry.

He was fast, she'd grant him that. But she had to make that call before he did. Panting, she stopped and tapped her phone, praying that Lauren would pick up.

10

*E*ven when Junie locked her shop for the day, she was still fuming over Knox and his competitive bid against her. He didn't come by the shop, not that she expected him to.

That afternoon, Whitley sent out a memo asking everyone to meet an important new member of the team tomorrow. *Probably Knox.* Junie hoped she'd have a deluge of customers at the same time.

She had been nervous all day. Fortunately, she had reached Lauren and increased her offer, which was submitted right away. Lauren told her the sellers would review all offers tonight.

Junie parked the golf cart in her grandmother's driveway and walked to the front door.

Maileah met her at the door. "Hey, you're late."

"For what?"

"The surfing lesson you told me about before you left this morning." Maileah snapped her fingers in her face. "Earth to Junie. I got out of bed for this."

"Stop it, Maybelle," Junie said, just noticing that her sister had a swimsuit on under her jean shorts and tank top.

Junie was feeling depleted as she waited for the sellers to reply. Still, she had asked Maileah to be ready when she got home today. Sailor would be waiting for them at the beach. He'd told her they were only going to acquaint themselves with the boards and paddle around. Nothing fancy.

She could probably manage that, but she couldn't face anything more strenuous. The encounter with Knox had sapped her energy.

"I'll change and be right back." Junie tapped a message to Sailor.

As she was heading toward her mother's old room— now that her sister was in the guest room—her grand-mother stopped her in the hallway.

"Darling, why the long face?" Ella placed a hand on Junie's cheek. "I thought you were excited about your offer on Mrs. Ashbury's Sunshine Avenue house. Wasn't it accepted?"

"I haven't heard yet, Nana. But there's a competing offer from a man named Knox that Ryan just hired at the Majestic. I met him at the gift shop. I liked him at first, but as it turns out, he's horrible. And what sort of a name is Knox?"

"Scottish, I believe."

At least she'd gotten that part right, Junie thought miserably.

"I'm so sorry," Ella said. "When will you know which offer has been accepted?"

"Tomorrow, I hope."

"I'll hold good thoughts for you," Ella said. "I predict you'll find exactly what's right for you."

Junie rubbed her throbbing temples. "Lauren said something like that, too."

"She's an experienced real estate agent. That's why I suggested her, dear. Now, I understand you and Maileah are meeting Sailor at the beach. Don't keep him waiting too long." She lowered her voice. "I'm glad you're doing this for Maileah. Maybe he has a friend for her. You could double date."

Junie smiled at that. "You don't miss anything, do you, Nana?"

"I try not to." Ella hugged her. "Off you go now."

Her grandmother's words lifted her spirits, and Junie felt better. Being in the water always helped, too. She used to swim regularly, but she'd stopped after Mark died. Fortunately, her mother had given her a new swimsuit. She slipped into her room to change and pulled a T-shirt over it.

When she emerged, Maileah was still standing by the door. The two set off in the golf cart again. Within a few minutes, Junie pulled alongside the beach where Sailor was waiting.

Maileah leaned forward with sudden interest. "Is that Sailor?"

"Sure is."

"Hey, you two," Sailor called out. He had three boards leaning against his van.

"Sorry we're late," Junie said, swinging from the golf cart. She left her flip-flops behind.

"It's cool. I was just chillin' here." Sailor grinned and greeted her with a kiss on the cheek. "You're worth waiting for."

The sand was warm on her feet. Junie held out a hand. "This is my sister, Maileah."

"Hey," Maileah said. After peeling off her T-shirt and shorts, she sauntered toward them in her barely-there bikini. "Why are you called Sailor and not Surfer?"

Sailor laughed. "Because that's my name."

"Seriously?" Maileah said. "Not a nickname?"

"Nope." He smiled at Junie. "Usually, people ask if I sail."

Maileah stepped toward him. "And do you?"

Junie noted the flirtatious note in Maileah's voice, but she wasn't sure if Sailor picked it up. Maybe he was used to that and simply ignored it. However, Junie wouldn't.

"Sure," he replied. "Sailing is a lot of fun, too. There's plenty to do on Crown Island. Hiking, biking, hang gliding. Or you could go diving or snorkeling. There's another world below the surface."

"I hadn't planned on seeing it today," Maileah said, looking doubtful.

Sailor laughed. "This is a beginner-friendly spot for surfing. You'll be fine." He gestured toward the surfboards and hoisted one under his arm. "Take a board, and let's go."

"That's it?" Maileah asked.

"Don't worry. I'll show you what to do." He jogged ahead of them.

"I bet you could," Maileah said under her breath.

"What did you just say?" Junie asked, slightly irritated.

Maileah shrugged. "Nothing."

"Sailor asked me to the fireworks this weekend," Junie said pointedly. "Besides, I thought you were in mourning over Hawk."

"Hawk who?"

"Don't get snarky on me again," Junie said, pleading with her sister. "We just made up."

Maileah spread her hands. "I'm not doing anything. You're the one who didn't tell me you guys were seeing each other." She paused. "Do you think he's the one for you? Because if he's not…"

"It's a practice date, okay?" Junie took a surfboard. "Just behave." She was still upset over Knox and worried about the house. She wasn't in the mood for Maileah's tricks.

They trotted toward the water. After they stretched, Sailor showed them the basics of how to attach the leash to an ankle so they wouldn't lose their board. He also taught them how to sit and balance on the board and how to paddle to where small waves were breaking.

"You have to read the ocean," Sailor said. "Be aware of tides and rip currents. Every coastline is different, and sandbars can shift. Watch the winds, too. Light offshore winds are better for clean breaking waves. Gusty winds make choppy waves."

"Do I have to get up early to surf?" Maileah asked.

Sailor laughed. "Dawn is a good time to catch those light offshore winds, but the late afternoon and early evenings work, too. Like now."

Junie watched her sister closely. Maileah had scaled back on her flirting, but she was still watching Sailor very closely. But then, of course she would. He was their instructor.

She sighed. Maybe she was being too sensitive, but this wouldn't be the first time her sister had flirted with Junie's boyfriends.

Paddling over the waves, Junie corrected herself. Not that Sailor was her boyfriend. Not yet anyway. Considering that possibility, she wiped saltwater from her face and blinked. She and Sailor often talked at the hotel and took breaks together. She liked him well enough. Maybe even a little more than that. And she was a lot more comfortable with Sailor than Blue.

Which reminded her that she had to talk to Sailor about their fireworks date.

Still, even as she thought about that, a twinge of guilt gathered in her chest. She recalled her therapist's advice. *Guilt is perfectly normal. You'll get past that.*

Junie wondered if she would. Instead, she tried to relax. She focused on the waves and enjoyed the feeling of being in the water again. There really was a therapeutic motion to the ocean's swells, a constancy and energy that filled her with awe and respect.

Sailor looked at ease in the water, while Junie felt small on this vast ocean. Yet, the sea also filled her with a sense of power. If she could ride the waves like Sailor, it must feel like such an accomplishment. As if she could do anything she set her mind to.

Just then, Junie spied a larger wave coming toward them. Maileah and Sailor were chatting and didn't see it. "Watch out," she cried.

Sailor took it easily, but the wave crested and broke over Maileah. She slipped off her board and came up coughing. Her hair was drenched and covering her face.

Instantly, Junie's heart pounded, and she started toward her to help her. But Sailor was there beside her, patting her on the back and smoothing her hair back.

"Hey, you're okay," he said, grinning. "That was a small one."

"Really?" Maileah sputtered.

Sailor chuckled. "That's probably enough for today. Let's head back."

Once they reached the shore, Sailor took their boards, and Maileah flopped onto the sand.

Junie returned with the striped beach towels she'd left in the cart. She tossed one to her sister and sat beside her. "What did you think about surfing?"

"Except for nearly drowning, it's kind of fun," Maileah replied. "And Sailor…"

Junie shot her a look of warning.

"Okay, you win. I won't steal your boyfriend."

"He's not my boyfriend."

"Then what is he? A boyfriend in training?"

Junie nudged her. "I don't think he's the trainable type."

Sailor strolled back and joined them. "Want to do this again?"

"That was fun," Junie said. "We're in."

"Cool," Sailor said. "And are you in for the fireworks show?"

"I'd like that," Junie said, clasping her hands around her knees. Her chest tightened in discomfort, but she told herself she'd get past it.

They talked for a while, watching the sun slip toward the horizon, until Maileah began shivering.

"Here you go." Sailor put a dry towel around her. "You'll get used to the water. Or you could wear a wetsuit."

"Would you help me find one?" Maileah asked.

"We should go," Junie said, interrupting her. "I'm expecting a call."

Sailor looked up. "I heard you put an offer in on the house across from Jo."

"You heard?" Junie was anxious to hear from Lauren about the offer.

"It's Crown Island," Sailor said, shrugging. "Hard to keep a secret here."

"I've noticed. Lots of rumors, too." Junie thought about her mother and Ryan. People thought they were having an affair before they even started dating.

Sailor looked between them. "That house is a wreck. If you need help painting or anything before you guys move in, let me know. I could get some guys to help."

"Maileah isn't moving in with me," Junie said, dreading the thought. "But I'll keep that in mind."

"You know, that's not a bad idea," Maileah said. "I could help you until I figured out what I'm going to do. It's probably time we gave Nana's house back to her and Mom."

"You just got there," Junie said.

"But you've been here for months. Maybe she's tired of guests."

"Nana had pneumonia. We were helping her."

Maileah shrugged. "Okay, but it's still a good idea, don't you think? We could throw some parties. Wouldn't that be cool?"

While Junie might be uncomfortable living alone for a little while, she would get used to it. She didn't want Maileah around all the time, and her sister often left messes in her wake. Literally and figuratively. And if what she'd heard about Hawk from her mother and Deb was an indication of Maileah's taste in men, she didn't want her sister inviting strangers to her house.

"I really need some peace and quiet," Junie said.

"Fine. Have it your way." Maileah stood. "Hey Sailor, could I get a ride back to the house?"

"Sure, but—"

"You're coming with me, Maybelline," Junie said, scrambling to her feet. She hooked her arm through her sister's. "Let's talk tomorrow, Sailor."

When they were out of earshot of Sailor, Junie said, "You're still a brat. I thought you'd changed."

"I'm trying," Maileah said. "But he's really cute, and did you see how concerned he was when I nearly drowned? Hawk was nothing like that."

"You weren't anywhere near drowning. You just got your hair wet."

"That's practically the same thing." Maileah stuck out her lower lip.

"You promised, Mayday."

"Okay, I'll back off. I was just trying to have a little fun. Isn't that what everyone wants me to do?"

"Not at someone else's expense."

They got into the golf cart, and Junie started it. "Why do you keep doing stuff like that?"

Maileah bit her lip. "I'm not like you. But I'm trying to be. It's just that…that's the only way I know how to get attention." She sounded defeated. "You remember how Dad was. Everything was a game with him."

"Sometimes I wish I could forget." As Junie pointed the vehicle toward Beach View Lane, she reached out to Maileah, her heart softening toward her. "You can start over here. Be the person you want to be."

That went for her, too, Junie realized. But was Sailor the one for her? She pushed back her damp hair, feeling a little chagrined at herself. They hadn't even had their first date yet.

11

*K*nox followed Whitley into Ryan's office. A week ago, he wasn't sure if Crown Island would be a good fit for him and his family. But after what he'd seen here at the Majestic Hotel and in the community, he couldn't think of a better place to raise Penny. He thought his parents would like it, too.

"Have you made your decision, Knox?" Ryan rose from his massive desk at the Majestic. He walked around to the front and leaned against it. He had a healthier look than when Knox had worked with him in New York. Or maybe it was the casual Hawaiian shirt Ryan wore.

"I've given it a lot of thought," Knox replied.

"Want me to leave you two alone?" Whitley asked.

Ryan gestured to Knox. "Your call."

Knox drew a deep breath. "Since I'm joining the team, you might as well stay."

"That's my man," Ryan said, clapping him on the back. "Your project management skills are critical for this renovation. Whitley and I are already maxed out. You'll enjoy working with Deb Whitaker, the interior designer."

"I like what she's done so far," Knox said. "And I look forward to meeting her, too."

Whitley beamed and shook his hand. "Welcome aboard. When can you start?"

"Today, if you want. My parents will take care of Penny and the move." Knox had already discussed this with his parents, and they had agreed that the less they moved, the better. "I can fly back for a couple of days to finalize plans with them."

"Did you find a place to live?" Ryan asked.

Knox nodded, pleased with his progress so far. "My offer on a house on Sunshine Avenue has been accepted. I also have an offer on another house on the same block for my parents. My real estate agent is confident it will be accepted, given the circumstances. I wrote a letter to the estate attorney outlining the situation and explaining why I'm the right buyer for it."

"That's a good move," Ryan said. "Emotions often come into play when there are comparable offers."

"That's what I'm counting on."

"About that suit," Ryan said, gesturing to the dark suit Knox wore. "The only one wearing a jacket around here is Whitley. He's got the rainbow covered."

"The better for people to spot me," Whitley said, touching the lapel of his peacock blue jacket. "It's my trademark, so to speak."

"Get yourself some casual trousers," Ryan said. "We supply these aloha shirts for the staff, or you can wear your own. We want our guests to relax from the moment they step inside the Majestic."

"The staff likes the new look," Whitley added.

"I'll bet they do," Knox said. "I'll slap some stickers on my hard hat as well."

"That's the spirit," Ryan said, gesturing toward a table with several chairs around it. "You can stay here until you get moved. Now, let's get to work. I'd like you to take over the construction schedule right away. I know you're up to it."

Knox dove into the project, and by the time he finished with Ryan and Whitley, he was famished. He wanted to change clothes before going to the cafe at the hotel, but first, he wanted to call his parents and share his good news. He headed down the stairs toward his room, loosening his tie as he went.

Junie was crossing the lobby, carrying packages for a customer. He held back, avoiding her. She was easily one of the most unpleasant women he'd ever met. Who left someone by the side of the road and whizzed off in a golf cart?

She had bid against him on the house, he surmised. But he was certain his offer would be accepted. He had always prided himself on his persuasive abilities when he put his mind to it.

Arriving at his room, he went inside, immediately shedding his tie and jacket. He'd pick up a shirt downstairs in the employee quarters later. That would do for now.

Knox kicked off his shoes, untucked his shirt, and eased his large frame onto the bed. He tapped his phone to call his parents.

When his mother answered, he said, "I have great news, Mom."

"Did you get the job?" Wanda asked.

"I started today," Knox said with pride. "Are you and Pops ready to move?"

"We sure are. And Penny is so excited. She's been drawing palm trees and beaches since you left. Hold on, I'll call Doug." His mother muffled the phone and called his father.

The MacKenzie family was small; Knox was their only child. His parents made up for Lola's absence as much as they could, and Knox thought they did a fine job of it. But as Penny grew older, he worried that she would miss having a mother to confide in. Yet he was uneasy about dating and making another mistake.

It often happened that just when a woman caught his attention, he'd realize they had serious personality flaws. Like that Junie woman, who was easily one of the rudest women he'd ever met.

Maybe she thought the same about him. He'd have to keep his distance at the Majestic. While she worked in the gift shop now, she was probably the sort that wouldn't stay in a customer-facing job long. Not with her personality.

Satisfied, he waited for his father.

"Congratulations, son," Doug MacKenzie bellowed.

Knox grinned. His father had a boisterous personality and had been awarded a Purple Heart medal during his Naval career. He still had the shrapnel scars to show for it. His mother had been a journalist, and they had met during the war in Afghanistan. While Doug MacKenzie would never run track again as he had in high school, he didn't let that stop him from living life as well as he could.

Knox's parents were his heroes, and he willingly shouldered the obligation to help provide for them.

"Dad, I've got incredible news for you."

"Have you found some of my missing parts?" Doug chuckled at his own joke.

"Even better. How would you and Mom like to live in paradise with me and Penny?"

His father fumbled the phone and shouted, "Wanda, start packing! We're moving to Crown Island with the boy."

Holding the phone away from his ear, Knox laughed. "Let me tell you about the job, and this great house I'm buying." Another call beeped, but Knox sent it to voice mail. This was too important to interrupt.

Knox had so much to tell his parents. "And for you and Mom, there's another house on the same block, plus a garden in between. They'll need some work, but I'll get you some help on that." He was so confident that he told his father everything. "I'll fly out soon to sort out things."

"We'll manage just fine with Penny," Wanda said, piping up.

They spoke for a while, and by the time Knox hung up, he was feeling as excited as they sounded.

As far as he was concerned, the only blemish on the island was Junie. He tried to get her out of his mind. It wasn't like him to let someone like that disturb him.

12

Maileah sauntered into the kitchen, her mind still on Sailor. Even though she hadn't wanted to take surfing lessons initially, Sailor was easygoing —and awfully cute. Idly, she wondered if she had a chance with him. If Junie wasn't interested in him.

Her grandmother looked up from the local newspaper she was reading. "How were the surfing lessons?" Ella asked, looking over the rims of her reading glasses.

"Pretty good," Maileah replied, hoping she sounded sufficiently nonchalant. "Junie was right. Splashing around in the ocean felt good."

"Must have been good exercise," Ella said, slowly turning a page. "I haven't seen you look this good since you arrived. Sailor is a champion surfer, but how is he at teaching?"

"He's good. And he practically saved me from drowning."

"Good heavens!" Ella's brow creased with concern. "What happened?"

Maileah told her the story, giving it a touch of dramatic embellishment.

"And he carried you all the way to shore?" Ella asked when Maileah finished.

"Well, only a few steps to the shallow part," Maileah said, backing off the story. "I don't know that Junie saw that part."

"That's quite the story," Ella said, pulling out a chair for her.

"I guess it is." Maileah grinned, recalling how they used to make up stories about pirates and mermaids when she was younger.

Maileah had always looked forward to visiting her grandmother, though now she felt guilty that she hadn't returned much in recent years. She figured she was making up for it now. Still, she didn't belong here. She didn't know where she belonged anymore.

Ella smoothed the paper and looked up at her. "Are you going out today?"

Maileah had hardly been out except for the surfing lesson. "I don't have anything to do."

"You could go for a walk on the beach," Ella said. "You might meet someone interesting or stumble across a job prospect. You never know what might happen until you get out there."

Maileah rested her chin in her hand. Unlike Junie, she needed to work but had no idea what she could do on the island. "I was thinking of going back to Seattle for work, but I don't want to run into Dad and Olga."

Ella removed her glasses. "Then stay here. You could work remotely or take the ferry across the bay. Plenty of people commute like that."

"I'd like to try something new," Maileah said. "I'm bored with technology marketing."

"Then ask around. See if you could find something here."

"But I don't know anyone."

"You know Sailor," Ella said with a smile. "Ask him. He knows a lot of people on the island."

Maileah sat up. "I could do that."

"Go see him today. He's probably running the bike concession at the Majestic Hotel."

"I'm not sure what I'd say. Starting over at my age is so hard."

Ella folded the newspaper and set it aside. "Just be yourself, dear. You're a smart, attractive young woman with so much to offer. As for starting over, lots of people remake themselves. Someday, you'll look back and wish you were this age again."

"But I'm already in my mid-thirties, and I have nothing," Maileah whined. "No home, no children, not even a relationship."

In Seattle, she'd been living an extended party life, but here on Crown Island, she saw clearly what was missing. So many questions were swirling in her mind. How fast could she catch up? Or worse, was it too late?

Ella touched her hand. "Before you second-guess yourself, go wash your face and brush your hair. You can be ready in ten minutes. Your decision to talk to Sailor today could change your life."

"But I haven't decided."

Ella laughed. "Stop making excuses, dear. Now go on. I know you're up for this. Look how far Junie has come since she arrived."

At the mention of her sister, Maileah's competitive nature edged out her doubts. She pushed back her chair and stood. "I guess I could."

"There's the strong-willed young woman I know," Ella said, clapping her hands. She leaned forward, her eyes gleaming. "Remember, you don't want to look like you're trying too hard. Wear something beachy, but not a bikini."

Maileah grinned at the fashion advice. "Thanks, Nana. I'll keep that in mind." She bent over to kiss her cheek.

BEFORE SHE HAD time to reconsider her decision, Maileah was outside, striding along the beach toward the Majestic Hotel. She'd managed to find a relatively clean tank top and cut-off shorts in her room. She didn't want to look like an outsider.

Straight ahead was Sailor's bike concession stand. The glint of sun on a row of shiny beach cruisers caught her attention, but what truly held her gaze was Sailor. His sun-bleached hair framed an equally sun-kissed face. He was lean, confident, and easygoing.

Maileah strolled over to the bike concession, her eyes fixed on Sailor, who was tinkering with a bike. She watched as he wiped the sweat off his forehead with the back of his hand, his muscles rippling in the mid-day sun.

She had meant to stop by the gift shop to see Junie, but she stood rooted to the spot, transfixed by Sailor. He chatted easily with a couple of guests and kids.

When he looked up and saw her, a slow smile spread across his face. "Hey there, Maileah," he said, wiping his hands on a rag. "Get any surfing in?"

"I need another lesson first," she said, returning his easy

smile. "I'm afraid a wave might knock me out, and you'd be nowhere around to save me."

"Smart girl."

Maileah blushed slightly. As much as she wanted to talk to him, she'd rather get him away from here so they could speak in private. Here, there would be too many interruptions. It was almost lunchtime. She wondered if he would take a break with her.

"Do you know where I can get a good burger?" she asked, trying to keep her voice steady. "Besides the Majestic, I mean."

A slight pang of guilt struck her. Junie might be going out with him to see the fireworks this weekend. But her sister hadn't seemed genuinely excited about the idea. Not the way Maileah's heart pounded every time she looked at Sailor.

Surely Junie won't mind if I just talk to him, Maileah reasoned. After all, her sister had urged her to get out.

Sailor looked up, surprise flickering on his face. "Definitely Cuppa Jo's. Best burgers and shakes on the island. Have you been there?"

Maileah blinked and smiled. "No, I haven't. I wouldn't even know how to get there. Could you show me the way sometime?"

"Sure." Sailor grinned. "It's almost lunchtime if you'd like to go now."

"That would be great," she said, trying to hide her excitement. "Is it within walking distance?"

She really didn't know. Except for walking the beach and occasionally going to the Majestic Hotel with her family, she'd been cloistered in her room.

"I brought my electric bike today," Sailor said. "You can hop on the back."

Maileah beamed. Maybe Nana was right. All she needed to do was get out there.

As they headed toward Cuppa Jo's on the bike, Maileah wrapped her arms firmly around Sailor's taut torso. Not only was he in great shape, but he was also everything she liked in a man. Strong, confident, and adventurous.

Though he was nothing like Hawk.

"So, why the sudden craving for burgers?" Sailor's voice broke through her thoughts.

"Can't a girl get hungry?"

Sailor laughed. "We're almost there."

As they stepped into the vintage ambiance of Cuppa Jo's, Maileah noticed a few people glancing their way, but she didn't know anyone. They slid into a booth across from each other.

A woman with short, dark hair was at the counter. "That's Jo, the owner," Sailor said, nodding to her.

Jo made her way toward them, sizing up Maileah as she did.

"This is Junie's sister, Maileah," Sailor said, introducing them.

Surprise registered on Jo's face, though she recovered quickly. "Want to see the menu? We have specials on the board, too. Today, it's an avocado chipotle burger with sweet potato fries."

"I'll have that," Sailor said.

"Same," Maileah added.

While Sailor finished their order, Jo's scrutinizing gaze landed on Maileah, her eyebrows slightly knitted. Finally, she asked, "Are you visiting or thinking of staying on Crown Island?"

"I'm looking for work here," Maileah said, realizing she was committing herself. "If you hear of anything, I'm available. I worked in marketing for a big tech company in Seattle, so I have plenty of skills."

"I'll keep that in mind," Jo said lightly. "I'd better put your order in." She turned and headed toward the kitchen.

Maileah wondered if Jo knew that Junie was going out with Sailor. She supposed this looked bad, her being with Sailor, but she'd make sure Junie understood. Maileah was looking for work, after all.

Looking at Sailor, she said, "Are there any tech companies on Crown Island?"

"We don't have many big businesses on the island," Sailor said. "The Majestic is the largest."

"I couldn't work there," Maileah said. "Not with Junie around."

"Don't you two get along?" Sailor asked.

"Sure we do," Maileah said lightly.

She wanted to get along with her sister, but they were often at odds. Maybe Maileah had been the bossy older sister, although she preferred the word assertive.

And maybe she had been a little jealous of Junie's near-perfect marriage when she couldn't even manage a boyfriend for more than a few months. Why had she always attracted the wrong sort of man? Junie made it look easy and effortless.

At a momentary loss for words, Maileah shifted in her seat across from Sailor.

"Junie is pretty cool," Sailor said. "My dad told me her

husband was hit by a taxi in London. That must have been rough."

"You have no idea."

When Junie's husband died, it was devastating to Maileah, too. He brightened every room he entered. Junie and Mark were a golden couple that everyone loved.

Except Calvin, of course. He'd been so hung up on Mark's lack of a college education, even though he was a near genius-level computer coder.

In every fairytale, a little rain must fall, Maileah figured.

Sailor leaned toward her, his blue eyes blazing into her. "It's good that Junie had you, your mom, and your grandmother. You all seem close. I understand why you'd want to stay here and find work."

"I suppose we are." Maileah smiled. She didn't hear that often, as she was the black sheep of the family. But she had her reasons.

If she had been tough on Junie, it was only so she wouldn't slip away. She was terrified of losing her sister to the dark depression that cloaked her for weeks, then months, then years. If anything had happened to Junie— she shuddered slightly even thinking about it—she would have blamed herself for not trying hard enough to save her. Everyone coddled Junie, but when that didn't work, Maileah shifted to tough love. That had always lit a fire in Junie's heart when they were kids.

But now, she didn't know how to shift that behavior between them. They'd had a breakthrough sharing their feelings the other day, but Maileah was having a hard time maintaining that. Old habits, she supposed.

And wouldn't you know it, Sailor had to come along.

Maileah stole a glance at his open-necked shirt and sucked in a breath.

"Are you okay?" Sailor asked, ducking for a glimpse of her lid-shrouded eyes.

"Ouch." Maileah slapped her hand to break the tension building in her chest. "Just a little bug of some sort." She shook her shoulders. "So, any other companies you can think of that might need an unemployed, mid-career person like me who'd rather be surfing?"

Sailor laughed. "There's a fruit packing company, the city government, and some law offices. A lot of people surf before work."

Maileah wiggled her toes with nervous energy under the table. "My grandmother says you're pretty good."

"It's my thing," Sailor said, shrugging with modesty. "I'd do it all the time if I could. When you're surfing, it's such a feeling of freedom, of being one with nature. The power of the sea is incredible. For me, there's nothing like it."

"When I go snow-skiing, I feel like that," Maileah said. She truly meant it. She used to take off and go skiing on her own so she wouldn't feel like she had to impress anyone.

Sailor's eyes lit with interest. "Where do you ski?"

"Since I lived in Seattle, I often went to Stevens Pass, but Whistler and Blackcomb mountains are my favorite."

"I have a lot of friends in Canada," Sailor said. "I've been to Vancouver and skied Whistler with them. It's really cool. Ever skied Colorado or Utah?"

"Mammoth in California," Maileah said.

They started talking about their love of sports, and Maileah relaxed into the conversation. She felt like she and

Sailor were really connecting. Still, she could feel Jo's eyes on her.

How well does Jo know Junie? Maileah thought, unease building within her.

This might not have been one of her better ideas, but it was only hamburgers at a diner. Still, for her family's sake, Maileah hoped she wasn't at the center of island gossip.

13

*W*hen the bell on her shop door jingled, Junie looked up from the display of thick beach towels she was rearranging. The shop wasn't officially open yet, but it was Whitley.

She wondered if he'd had a chance to talk to Ryan about her taking over the gift shop. Junie felt like her life was on hold until she heard about her offers on the house and the gift shop.

"Got a minute before you open?" Whitley asked.

"As long as we need," Junie replied. "Have you been able to present my idea to Ryan?"

"That's what we need to talk about." Though he was always professional, Whitley looked uncomfortable. "I sat down with Mr. Ryan, and I assure you, he gave it careful consideration."

Junie was ready for what she assumed was coming next. Her upbeat mood deflated a little, but she knew this wasn't an ordinary request. Yet she couldn't shake the feeling that something had to change.

The gift shop was a steady source of income, although thankfully, she didn't have to depend on it. But without a more significant challenge, the gift shop would no longer fulfill her creatively. She was beginning to feel restless.

"Sounds like my idea wasn't received very well. Was I a victim of my success?"

Whitley lifted one side of his mouth in a half-smile. "I'm afraid that might have been part of it."

"I might as well hear the other part, too," Junie said, folding her arms.

"You're a valuable asset to the team here at the Majestic," Whitley said. "We don't want to lose you. However, while Mr. Ryan is the CEO, he also has investors and a board he must answer to. Your request was reviewed by others on the team."

"Were the ones who nixed it?"

Whitley shifted, clearly struggling with this conversation. "I'm afraid that with our major renovation underway, management is not keen to trim any profit-making activities. I'm sorry, Junie."

"I once had a business, so I understand." Still, she was disappointed.

While Junie appreciated his kind words, she couldn't ignore the nagging feeling in her gut. She had been depressed for so long after Mark's death. She finally felt like she wanted to lift off again and embrace a challenge. He would have wanted her to do that.

Still looking uncomfortable, Whitley jingled a set of keys in his pocket. "You and Ella and April are like family, so please know this decision is difficult for me, too. It grieves me to see your energy and talent stunted. The way you turned around the gift shop was remarkable."

"I care about people," Junie said. "That's what I do. Solve problems and serve happiness."

"You're doing that and more," Whitley said with compassion. "We've been lucky to have you."

It all started when Junie went to lunch at the hotel with her mother. She was in the gift shop when a bored clerk refused to help a customer. The woman needed clothing for her children after the airline misplaced their luggage. Junie felt the woman's frustration and jumped in to help.

After Whitley fired the clerk, she took another leap and applied for the position. It was a small, though important, step in her recovery. It had been a few months, so she was ready for the next step.

"I need more than just this," Junie said, waving her hand around the shop. "I've loved transforming the merchandise assortment, but I need more of a challenge."

Whitley sighed. "I hate to lose you here at the Majestic. Guest feedback on you and the shop has been excellent." Whitley glanced over his shoulder.

Junie sensed there was more he wanted to say. "Yes?"

"You didn't hear this from me," Whitley began. "But given the relationship between your mother and Mr. Ryan—"

"I'd rather not use that," Junie interjected. "I like to get ahead on my own merit."

"Of course, and you do." Whitley turned up a palm. "But at times, you do what you must."

"I should talk to Ryan directly?"

"I didn't say that, but that's an excellent idea." Whitley gave her a smile of encouragement. "You're a young woman who shouldn't give up easily."

"It was once an attractive option," Junie said. "But

being here at the Majestic has given me a fresh start. Whatever I decide to do, I won't leave you hanging."

"I appreciate that. And I know you'll make the right decision. I'll be rooting for you. Let me know how it goes."

After Whitley left, Junie turned over the cardboard sign on her shop that read, *Gone to the Beach.* She was open for business.

But for how long? This shop had literally saved her life. She'd come through the darkness after her husband's death, through endless days when she prayed to join him but didn't have the heart to do that to her family.

Even to Maileah, who was often merciless in her prodding.

Still, it was only a shop. It would go on without her. As Nana often told her and Maileah, *If you can't push through a wall of problems, climb over, tunnel under, or go around them. Sunshine is on the other side.*

And speaking of sunshine, she wondered when Lauren would call. It was all Junie could do not to contact her real estate agent every ten minutes. Lauren had promised to reach her as soon as she heard something.

The morning seemed to drag on and on. Several guests came in, and Junie made some good sales, but every time she checked her messages, there was nothing from Lauren.

Finally, she could wait no longer. She tapped a message. *Any word yet?* She stared at her phone, willing a reply.

The reply was swift. *Not yet. I checked a few minutes ago.*

Junie blew out a sigh. This was a good time for lunch. She flipped the sign and signaled to Faye across the hall. Her friend gave her a thumbs-up and flipped hers, too. She joined her in the hallway.

"Have you heard anything about the offer yet?" Faye asked.

"Soon, I hope."

The two women made their way downstairs to the employee break room. Even though Faye wasn't technically an employee, she had leased her space at the Majestic for so long that she was welcome there.

Junie spied Sailor talking to Whitley and a small throng of people. She heard introductions.

"Let's see what's up," Faye said, joining the group.

Junie followed, and Whitley turned toward her.

"Junie and Faye, I'd like you to meet the newest member of the Majestic Hotel family. Knox MacKenzie will oversee the renovation. You're sure to see him around."

Whitley turned to Knox. "Junie manages the gift shop, and Faye leases the space across from her."

Knox swung around, registering her with cool regard.

"Welcome to the Majestic," Junie managed to say, wishing she could evaporate.

"Junie," Knox said, dipping his head.

She could feel the chill from five feet away.

"Knox will visit your shop regarding the renovations needed in that space," Whitley said. "I'd like you to make notes for him about anything else you think might be required."

"Of course," Junie said, trying to maintain a pleasant tone in front of Whitley and Sailor, but all she wanted to do was strangle him.

"Where are you staying, Knox?" Sailor asked.

Knox quickly turned away from Junie. "I just bought a home on Sunshine Avenue."

"Cool," Sailor said. "Hey, Junie will be your neighbor.

She's buying a house there, too. Old Mrs. Ashbury's home. Did you buy the house on the corner?"

Knox nodded. "And the other one."

Junie's heart fell, and Faye touched her arm. "Oh, Junie, I'm so sorry. I know how much you wanted that house."

Sailor looked from Knox to Junie and quickly grasped the situation. "Aw, crickets. You guys were bidding on the same house?"

"I suppose we were." Junie lifted her chin, though keeping the disappointment from her face was hard. Two tough defeats in one day were almost more than she could handle.

She knew Sailor could see the frustration etched on her face. The house meant a lot to her, and it was hard for her to let it go, especially to Knox. He was sure to gloat over it.

Junie had imaged that she and Jo would pop into each other's house like Lucy and Ethel on the old *I Love Lucy* reruns she'd grown up with. She thought of the block parties and potluck dinners Jo had talked about and how eager her friend was to introduce Junie to others and help her spruce up the old house.

"There are other houses out there," Sailor said, putting his arm around Junie's shoulder. "Guess this one didn't have your name on it. Let's chill on the beach tonight. We can figure something out."

"I'll meet you there." Junie managed a weak smile. Sailor was probably right, but it still hurt.

Knox stood by awkwardly, watching them.

This was painful, but Junie had overcome greater losses. *It's only a house,* she thought, yet it represented much more than that. She refused to let Knox see how upset she was. With a determined look, she turned to him.

"I hope you enjoy the house and garden," she said, perhaps sharper than she'd meant.

Knox lifted one side of his mouth. "It's for my parents," he said, holding her in his magnetic gaze. "I'm sorry it didn't work out for you."

"Right." She was at a loss for words at his response.

He was likely faking that response for his new colleagues, but Junie let it go. At the thought of being so close to owning a home, anger and sadness surged through her.

But the house was gone. *And to him, of all people.* She blinked hard. She wouldn't let Knox see her cry.

"I'll find another place," she said, forcing a smile at Sailor. "Like you said, probably one even better."

Sailor gave her a sympathetic look, and Faye squeezed her arm. Junie took a deep breath and turned to leave. Her appetite had vanished.

But as she walked away, she couldn't help feeling a twinge of regret. What if she had bid just a little bit higher? Would she be the one holding the keys to that house right now?

Knox caught up with her. "Hey, Junie. You might not believe me, but I am sorry about the house. I know what it must have meant to you."

Junie looked at him, surprised that he would say that. She had expected him to wallow in his win or make a snarky remark. But, of course, it was only an act for his new coworkers.

She simply shook her head, afraid if she responded to that, she'd break down. Instead, she said, "Let me know when you want to inspect the shop."

"I will."

She turned from him and, with a determined stride, walked from the break room and hurried toward the ladies' room.

After Junie pushed the door open to the old, luxuriously furnished anteroom, she collapsed on one of the old fainting couches from the last century. Deb had marked these pieced for refurbishment, but Junie welcomed the old, musty smell, comforting as it was.

She pressed her fingers to her eyes, trying to stem her tears. This morning, her dreams and aspirations had seemed poised for fruition, but in the stark light of the hot afternoon, none of it was to be. She took a tissue and blew her nose. Feeling sorry for herself wouldn't solve anything.

Just then, her phone buzzed, and she glanced at it. It was Lauren.

Junie didn't feel up to rehashing what had happened. She knew, and that was all that mattered. She'd call Lauren later to thank her for her work, but right now, she needed to return to work and take her mind off all that had happened.

Swallowing her grief, Junie turned off her phone, splashed her face with water, and returned to the gift shop.

14

"*I*'ve been trying to reach you," Lauren said. "Was your phone off?"

"I couldn't speak." Junie sighed and turned away from the shop.

All afternoon, she'd thrown herself into cleaning and organizing to take her mind off her disappointment. Only now had she turned on her phone.

"You put a lot of work into this deal for me, Lauren. I'm sorry it didn't work out."

"What are you talking about?" Lauren said. "I'm calling to congratulate you."

"On what?" Junie was confused. "I didn't get the house."

She could still see Knox's face in her mind. That he intended the house for his parents eased her pain a little. Not much, but some. She imagined them as an older couple who needed help, and her heart went out to them. Knox might be an arrogant jerk, but at least he took care of his parents.

Lauren's laughter rolled over the phone line. "I don't know where you get your information, but I have a signed agreement in my hand. The sellers liked your cash offer and ability to close quickly. Your extra bid edged out the other offer, too. The house on Sunshine Avenue is yours, Junie."

A surge of excitement coursed through her, and Junie screamed with joy, dropping her phone in the process. Her dream of having a home again had come true, and she could hardly believe it.

Faye raced across the hall from her shop. "Are you okay?"

"I got the house," Junie cried, bouncing. "But I dropped my phone."

"Here it is," Faye said, scooping it up. "That's fantastic. I'm so happy for you."

"Are you still there, Lauren?"

Laughing, the real estate agent asked, "Are you okay?"

Pressing a hand to her pounding heart, Junie caught her breath. "I still can't believe it. There's a guy at work, and he thinks it's his."

"Believe it, Junie." Lauren chuckled. "There were other offers, but yours came out on top. I can hardly wait to see what you do with it."

"This is the best thing that's happened to me in a long time," Junie said. "Thank you for seeing it through, Lauren."

Owning a house was not just a financial investment. It was a symbol of her independence and a new chapter in her life.

"I'll bring the final paperwork to the hotel," Lauren said, giving her a few details.

Overwhelmed with emotions, Junie finally hung up the phone. She would have something to celebrate tonight, after all.

Faye stood beside her, fluttering her hands. "When do you get the keys?"

"In about a week," Junie replied. How quickly this had happened.

"You have to have a housewarming party right away."

Junie laughed. "That will be a house cleaning and painting party first. And I must get furniture. A bed, at least."

She figured her mother's friend Deb could help her or point her in the right direction for furnishings. And her mother always seemed to know the best antique shops.

"I'll help, too," Faye said, her eyes sparkling with excitement. "I'll help you get some guys together, like Blue and Sailor, and we'll knock that out in no time. I'm happy to watch the shop for you, too."

"You're being pretty optimistic."

"That's how we do things here," Faye said with a wink. "All you have to do is buy supplies and feed them. A stack of pizzas, a case of beer, and you're good to go."

Junie hugged her. "I have my eye on some things in your shop for the house."

"I'll give you a good deal," Faye said, grinning.

"What's this?" April appeared at the entry. "I had lunch with Ryan, and as I was leaving, I heard a scream down the hallway. It sounded like you."

"Oh, Mom, I got the house!" Junie flung her arms around her mother.

"Why, that's wonderful," April said, rocking back and

forth with her daughter. "Your grandmother will be thrilled that you're so close."

"I can walk or bike to Nana's and pick up things at the store for her. It will be so easy to drop off anything she needs."

With a look of pride on her face, April clasped her hands. "That's thoughtful of you, sweetheart."

"And I can hardly wait to decorate how I want." Ideas filled Junie's mind. "I'll have a guest bedroom and a craft room—or maybe an office. Fresh fruits and vegetables from the garden and potluck parties every week. At last, I'll be living the life I want again. Just without Mark."

This time, she would be on her own. She'd have to adjust, but her grandmother had lived alone for years after her beloved husband died. Junie would manage, too. Wishing it were otherwise was fruitless, she now realized.

They talked for a little while until Faye had to leave to help a customer in her shop.

"We can celebrate tonight," April said.

"How about the next day?" Junie suggested. "I'm going to the fireworks on the beach tonight."

"I've heard that's quite an event." April pressed a finger to her lips in thought. "I should ask Ryan. He'd probably enjoy that. Who are you going with?"

"Blue asked me, but I'm trying to put him and Jo back together. They were serious at one time, but Jo got cold feet, and she regrets it now. I think Blue asked me out only because he is trying to get over her. I understand how he probably feels."

April frowned. "Are you sure that's a good idea? They might have some other problems."

Junie hadn't thought about that, though it was a possibility. "Jo is going, so I'm just giving them the opportunity. They're both adults, so if they want to figure out their relationship, they will."

"That's considerate of you. If it's right for them, I hope it works out."

Junie was looking forward to watching the fireworks. Blue would pick her up for dinner, but she had arranged to meet Sailor there a little later.

If all went well, Junie would be left with Sailor at the end of the evening. He was a nice enough guy, people said. She'd give him a chance.

Junie noted the time. "I should close the shop now. If you walked, I'll give you a lift home."

"That would be nice," April said. "Want to see the progress on the historical society space? It's really being transformed. Deb and her crew have put a huge amount of work into it."

"I'd like that." After Junie locked the door, they walked across the Majestic Hotel grounds to the historical society office, which had once been a dance hall.

April opened the door, revealing an in-progress construction zone. The old wooden floors were covered with paper and tarps to protect them. A fine layer of dust covered everything.

"Deb's vision is coming together." Her mother gestured toward the open beamed ceiling. "We removed the ceiling and exposed the rafters, so it feels much airier."

"And you opened the front of the building. Wow." Junie walked through, admiring the changes. "You'll bring in more foot traffic from Orange Avenue. That will be good for business."

"I'll put a couple of bistro tables and chairs on the front

walkway," April said. "Painting begins next week, and Deb is ready to move in furnishings the week after. It will come together quickly. And then the real historical work begins."

"How is that?" Junie asked.

Her mother smiled. "I'm planning a timeline for that wall, as well as exhibits on Crown Island founders, the Majestic Hotel developers and guests of note, and environmental aspects." She raised her hand to the wall. "The sea, the beaches, the preservation of wildlife species. And so much more. We'll also feature the Princess Noelle necklace you found and other historical artifacts I've discovered in the hotel and other places."

"You really love the history of this island," Junie said with admiration. "I'm glad you found a niche to fill here, Mom."

Junie was genuinely impressed with what her mother had done. From conceiving the idea and raising funds to putting it into action, April had been the driving force. If her mother could do that, so could she.

"I'm proud of what you've done here, Mom. We were all worried about you when Dad spun out of control. But look at you now. You're an inspiration."

April put her arm around Junie. "No one goes through life without adversity. Difficulties often arise when you least expect them. How you respond determines the kind of person you are or will become—someone who rises to challenges or folds into victimhood."

"It took me a while to come around," Junie admitted. At her darkest hour, she had lost the will to live.

April kissed her cheek. "Trials of the heart are the hardest. You're doing just fine now, and I know Mark would be proud of you."

Junie blinked against the sudden tears that sprang to her eyes. Even now, he had hold of her heart. Maybe he always would. But there was something else troubling her.

"Mom, do you think I'll ever have the capacity to love again? I wanted children with Mark, and I still do. But I don't know if I could ever love another man as I loved him."

April leaned against the edge of a table. "Just as no two people are alike, no two loves are alike. I'm growing to care more for Ryan every day. And I loved your father in the beginning. A part of me still loves the man he was then. Yet, Calvin has become someone I don't recognize. Love changes as we mature, darling. We value different traits."

"I want a family, but I don't want to rush into anything," Junie said thoughtfully. "I'm considering the alternatives. Maybe adopting an older child. But I'm not sure yet."

April took Junie's hands. "When you're ready, you'll know it's right."

"That sounds like what I told Maileah the other day."

"Then you already know."

Junie nodded slowly. "But it's easier to give advice than take it."

Her head was still swirling with excitement over the house, and Junie had a lot of work ahead of her. She wasn't sure if she would stay at the Majestic, either. Although she enjoyed the people she worked with—not counting Knox, of course—she wanted to be fully committed for the long term, whatever that might look like.

"Ready to go?" April asked.

Junie nodded, and her mother shut the door.

At home, Junie changed into a flowing aquamarine

sundress and loosely braided her hair to one side. By the time Blue arrived to pick her up, she was ready. She made her way into the living room to wait with Nana.

"You should come with us," Junie said to her.

"On your date?" Ella laughed. "I'm surprised you'd want a chaperone."

"It's not exactly a date," Junie said. But before she could elaborate, a knock sounded at the door, and Junie opened it.

Ella stood to greet Blue. "Why, it's so nice to see you out of uniform."

"Ma'am," Blue said with a slight bow. "You look lovely this evening, Miss Ella. And you, too, Junie."

As Junie greeted him, she noticed his smile seemed forced. It was pleasant enough, but it barely extended to his eyes. His mind was somewhere else. She could appreciate that. Still, he was going through the motions, even with a broken heart.

She hoped she could help him mend that.

"I know it's early for dinner," Blue began.

Sensing his awkwardness, Junie asked, "Would you rather eat at the beach? I heard some food trucks will be there."

His face relaxed with visible relief. "That's just fine."

Neither of them was looking forward to a stilted dinner conversation. "We'll be early, but we can walk on the beach," Junie said. "Maybe we'll see some friends. Faye said she was on her way."

Once they arrived, Junie kept an eye out for Jo. She hoped this plan would go well.

Blue waved at someone across the gathering crowd. "Have you met our newest resident, Knox MacKenzie? He's taken a job with Ryan at the Majestic."

Junie's heart fell. He was the last person she wanted to see. "Yes, I met him at work."

"I heard he bought that corner house on Sunshine Avenue. That's where you're looking, too, isn't it?"

She noticed he was careful not to mention Jo. "That's right."

"Then you'll be neighbors."

"I suppose so." She wasn't thrilled about that, but at least they had a garden separating them. She glanced around. Where on earth was Jo? Had she gotten cold feet again?

Junie tried to push the thought of Knox out of her mind, but he seemed to be everywhere she looked. She caught him staring at her a few times. Worse, she felt a strange pull toward him. She tried to focus on the festivities around her.

Gesturing at the food trucks, she said, "Tuna poke, barbecue, or vegan?"

"I like them all." Blue gazed longingly at the barbecue.

"I bet you're a carnivorous sort," she said. "I'm a pescatarian, but we can split up."

"Would you mind?" Once again, he looked relieved.

"I'll meet you at that picnic table over there." Walking toward the tuna poke truck, she spied Jo around the side. "Hey, you. I was getting worried."

"I'm sorry," Jo said, fidgeting. "But I don't know how he'll react."

"If you're with me, he can't run away. I'll leave you two to talk. We're going to meet at that far table."

The community had put out some folding tables. Many people had brought blankets to sit on the beach.

"Okay." Jo tugged at her dress. "Do you think this looks

okay? He bought it for me, but maybe wearing it was a bad idea."

"I think it's perfect."

Biting her lip, Jo said, "The music will start soon. I don't know if we can talk above that."

"Then take a walk." Placing a hand on Jo's shoulder, Junie added, "I'd give anything to see Mark again. But I'll never have that chance. You do. Make the most of it. You won't regret it, but if you don't try, you will."

"Thank you for doing this, Junie."

She hugged Jo. "You've got this."

They waited until Blue had sat down. With her food in one hand and Jo's clammy hand in the other, Junie wove toward Blue.

"Look who I found on the way," Junie said brightly.

Blue nearly dropped his drink. "Jo. What are you doing here?"

"I came to see the fireworks. Small town, right?"

"Well, I'm here with Junie now," Blue said awkwardly.

A meaningful look passed between them.

Junie looked down at her food. "Oh, my goodness. I think they gave me the wrong order. Why don't you two talk?"

"I'll return it for you," Blue said, quickly getting up from the table.

"That's okay," Junie said, backing up. "You and Jo might want to catch up. I'll be around if you need me."

Suddenly, Blue realized what was happening. Flexing his jaw, he said, "You set this up?"

"Just talk to her," Junie replied. "People change their minds, Blue. Do it for me?"

Slowly, he sat down, and Junie made her way toward

the food truck to wait. She was trying not to stare but couldn't help glancing in their direction.

Jo was leaning toward Blue and talking in earnest. He was nodding, and after a few minutes, he reached for her hand.

"Oh, thank heavens," Junie breathed.

They were going to be okay, at least for now. She figured she should look for Sailor now. She spied him across the crowd, talking to Maileah.

Junie was surprised. She hadn't even known that her sister planned to attend. Maileah was getting out, though, and that was good.

Turning, she caught Knox's eye. This time, he lifted his chin and began walking toward her.

15

*J*unie stood rooted to the spot. Clearly, Knox wanted to speak to her. Now that he was part of the Majestic Hotel management team, she couldn't run away, or worse, tell him what she really thought of him.

On second thought, maybe she should.

As he came closer, he called out to her. "Junie, got a minute?"

She would have to speak to him, at least for a few minutes, and then she could excuse herself and find Sailor. That was a good plan. She wasn't ready to be fired until she had a chance to talk to Ryan.

Not that Knox had that sort of power, but he would have influence.

Dusk was gathering now, and people were setting up lawn chairs or rolling out blankets. Nearby, Faye waved to her. She sat with other friends on beach blankets anchored with coolers. The fireworks display would begin after nightfall. This celebration of the founding of Crown Island was an annual party.

Faye yelled to her. "Come join us."

"In a minute," Junie answered, her heartbeat quickening.

Knox was a few paces away. She lifted a hand in acknowledgment, eager to get this over with. "What's up, Knox?"

"I wanted to congratulate you," he said, his gaze settling on her. "And apologize for making a stupid assumption."

"It's okay. No harm done." This time, she would take the high road.

Knox shook his head. "I don't know why I acted like that, other than I really thought I would win the deal. I guess I was projecting because it meant a lot to me."

Unsure what to make of that, Junie crossed her arms. "Did you come here to ask me to sell the house to you? Because if you did—"

"What? No, not at all. It's just that we got off to a poor start." Knox gave her a half-smile. "I realize we'll soon be neighbors, and I didn't want our competition to turn into an all-out war between us. Ryan and Whitley speak highly of you, so I thought I should give you another chance."

She hadn't expected this. His gaze was unwavering, and he was so close that she caught a faint whiff of his fresh cologne. Citrus and sandalwood, like one of the candles she carried. In the waning light, his hair looked like polished mahogany. It was still damp around the edges, curling a little on his neck.

She leaned in, feeling drawn to him. It was nice, she thought, surprised at the feeling.

"Can we be friends?" he asked, still staring at her.

Junie shook her head to dispel her trance-like state. "I'm sorry, but did you just say you wanted to give *me* another chance?"

"Ouch. I did, didn't I?" He ran his hand over his hair. "That should be the other way around. After what I thought about you, I'm the one who should be asking for a second chance."

Now, she was intrigued. "What were you thinking of me?"

Knox laughed uncomfortably. "I can't say."

"Oh, come on," she said, grinning.

"Let's just say we probably weren't thinking very highly of each other, and I'm sure I deserved all of it." Know rubbed his chin. "Can we rewind to the first day we met?"

"When you caught my phone? That was impressive. You have good reflexes." Junie allowed a small smile. Knox seemed different now. More relaxed. And wow, was he easy to look at.

She extended her hand. "Hi. I'm Junie, and I run the gift shop. Used to have an online shop, too."

He clasped her hand. "Ryan mentioned that."

Knox's voice held a slight sympathetic note that Junie had become accustomed to hearing. "That's not all he said, was it?"

"Uh, no. I'm really sorry for your—"

"Thank you," she said, cutting him off. She didn't want to think about Mark right now. "But it's time for me to move on now. That's why I'm buying the house."

"Me, too." Knox held her gaze. "You'll meet my daughter soon. The one you made the gift bag for. She really liked it, by the way."

"I'm glad. Where is she now?"

"In New Jersey with my parents. They help look after her, so you'll probably see them around. Especially my mother." Knox grinned. "She's a lot of fun, but she likes to know everyone's business. I apologize in advance."

Immediately, Junie was full of questions, even though his life wasn't any business of hers either. "Will your parents stay with you?"

"The house on the corner has two primary suites, so there is plenty of room for now. But I know my father. He'll want his own space." Knox grinned again. "He's an independent old fart."

Junie laughed at that description. "Something will probably come up for sale in the neighborhood. And I promise I won't be competing with you again. That house will be more than enough for me."

His expression turned serious, and he reached out to touch her hand. "You know it needs a lot of work, right?"

His touch sent a shiver through her. "And as it turns out, I have a lot of friends. Want to join the painting party?"

"I can do that," Knox replied, nodding. "My parents could probably help with the old garden. For a price, that is. You can pay in lemons and oranges."

"That's a deal," she said happily. "Jo told me Mrs. Ashbury always had plenty of fruit to share."

Junie paused, looking at Knox with fresh eyes. Maybe he wasn't such a jerk after all. "When will they arrive?"

"We're arranging that now," Knox replied, taking a step closer to her. "I'll fly back for a couple of days to organize the move. They'd like to come soon because the weather at home is still cold." He smiled, letting his gaze linger on her. "They're going to love it here."

Just then, firecrackers popped nearby. Junie turned to see a group of teenagers lighting sparklers on the beach. "I used to love those."

"So did I." Knox gestured toward the kids. "Bet I can talk them out of a couple."

Glancing over her shoulder, she saw Maileah and Sailor. They were still deep in conversation. At the picnic table, Blue sat with an arm around Jo, and she was resting her head on his shoulder. They both looked content.

She wasn't needed anywhere, she thought happily.

After talking to the kids, Knox returned, waving a pair of sparklers like a prize. He lit one and handed it to her. "For the kid in you."

She laughed and swung it in a slow arc like a glittery rainbow. "So pretty."

"But not as bright as you are," Knox said. Immediately, he backed off. "I didn't mean that like it sounded. It's a compliment."

Junie smiled at his awkward moment. "What a nice thing to say. Thank you."

The fire illuminated his hazel green eyes, and Junie was intrigued by the depth and intelligence she saw in him. When he looked at her, his gaze never wavered, and it sent chills through her. It seemed as if he were looking right into her soul. Yet, she wondered about his sincerity. Was he for real?

At once, a whizzing sound caught her attention. Looking up, she saw a stream of light split the night sky, shooting higher and higher until it burst into a waterfall of colors. The crowd gathered on the beach gasped in unison, applauding the start of the fireworks show.

Knox brushed off a rock. "We can sit here and watch if you'd like."

"You're being awfully neighborly." Junie eased onto the rock.

"I want us to get off to a good start this time around. How am I doing?"

"I don't know," she said, playfully nudging him. "I haven't seen your painting skills yet."

He laughed. "Look, there's another one." He looked up, watching the shower of fireworks raining over the waves.

Junie stared up, too. She liked the sound of his laughter and couldn't help stealing looks at him from the corner of her eye. This turn of events was surprising.

She had been intent on avoiding him, but now, she was enjoying his company.

The fireworks show lasted about twenty minutes. When it was over, people carrying sleepy children began to disperse. Older teens danced on the beach, and other people were still languishing on blankets, talking and laughing.

"I should go," Junie said, though she hated to prevail on Sailor or Blue for a lift home. "I open the shop early on Saturday mornings because that is the busiest day. That's when people realize they forgot their toothbrush or their luggage didn't make it."

"I could give you a lift home," Knox said. "I brought my rental car."

"I'd like that. Where are you staying?"

"At the hotel. Ryan has given me a room until my house closes escrow, which shouldn't take too long. The closing is running ahead of schedule."

"That's convenient for you."

"Especially since the construction crew at the hotel starts work early."

They walked toward his car in companionable silence, and Junie couldn't recall feeling so at ease with any man. Except her husband, but she still didn't want to think of him tonight.

She stole another glance at Knox and caught him doing the same. They laughed, and then their hands brushed. That touch was like a jolt of lightning, and she pulled her hand back as if she'd be burned.

Knox looked at her with a questioning expression, but he let it slide.

When they reached her grandmother's home, Junie stepped from the car, even as Knox hurried to open her door. "You don't have to do that," she said. "It's not as if we're dating or anything."

"My father's lessons are still with me," he said. Pausing, he gazed into her eyes again. "Goodnight, Junie. I'm glad we ran into each other and got a second chance."

"So am I," she said, inclining her head and letting her gaze fall to his lips. But only for a moment. Swiftly, she turned toward the door, wiggling her fingers in a small wave. He waited until she was inside the house.

Just as Mark had done. She couldn't help it. Junie passed a hand over her forehead, her feelings swirling with gale-like force.

16

Knox leaned toward his laptop monitor, chatting with his daughter Penny over video in his room at the Majestic Hotel. His time with her was usually the highlight of his day.

She looked so much like him with her coppery red hair, although she had her grandmother's bright blue eyes. Today, she wore a sparkly mermaid costume he'd sent to her.

At a break in her chatter about mermaids, he asked, "Are you excited about flying to join me on Crown Island soon?"

Penny looked uncertain. "With Grammy and Pops, too?"

"Of course. They'll live with us until we find them a house close enough so we can walk to visit."

Again, he wished his offer on the old house Junie bought had been accepted, but he was happy for her now. He had enjoyed talking to her a few days ago at the fireworks show on the beach. Junie was far different than he thought. What he had mistaken for competition turned out to be determination, and that he could respect. He had to develop that superpower himself after Lola left him with Penny.

"Lots of people were here packing boxes today," Penny said in her sweet singsong voice. "I kept out Tubbles and Monksey."

"Good. They'll want to travel with you." Knox hoped her stuffed animals wouldn't get lost on the way. "Keep them in your roller bag so they don't get lost." He'd bought a miniature one for her when he'd flown back to organize the move. He'd just returned.

"What's my room like?" Penny asked, bouncing on the couch.

"We'll decorate it however you want. Mermaids, pirates, or baby sharks?"

Penny wrinkled her nose. "You know what I like."

"Mermaids it is, then." He would order a set of mermaid sheets and pillows for her.

Penny's mouth turned down. "I'll miss my friends here."

"I know, but first grade is a big step." He wished he could hold her and comfort her. "You'll make new friends, for sure. I saw a girl about your age across the street. She seemed nice." He wanted to sound optimistic for her, but he was also concerned about her making friends in a small town where everyone knew each other.

"Really? Does she like mermaids?"

"I'll bet she does."

"Okay." Penny bounced again. "Bye, Daddy."

Knox put a hand on his heart. "I love you, Penny." She

was the little love of his life—and the reason he was moving to Crown Island.

"I love you, too, Daddy." She whisked out of the screen, singing to herself.

His mother came back onto the screen, wearing one of her wacky T-shirts with a fuzzy teddy bear and matching earrings. His mother had always been fun and outspoken. She might not have much of a verbal filter, but she made up for that with a huge heart.

"There she goes, dancing through life," Wanda said. "I'm sorry I can't get her to stay longer."

"That's okay. How's Dad doing?"

"The cold bothers his legs, you know."

Knox nodded. His father had a lot of shrapnel wounds, which bothered him in freezing temperatures and contributed to other health issues. That was part of the reason Knox had taken this job. But Doug McKenzie seldom complained.

"Wanda, are you talking about me again?" His father limped into view. "Hi, son. I'm fit as a fiddle, don't you worry."

"A fiddle short of a few strings," Wanda said. "Sit down and talk to your son. Don't make me duct tape you to that chair."

Knox smiled at that. His mother's zaniness probably stemmed from how she handled the stress of his father's lengthy military deployments.

He missed his parents, but they would arrive soon. Ryan had given him a sign-on bonus from the Majestic that Knox put toward the new house. As part of his compensation package, the moving allowance covered the cost of packing, transportation, and set up. His parents wouldn't have to do a thing except direct the movers. His mother could certainly do that.

Whitley had extended an employee discount for rooms at the Majestic, so his family could fly out to join him as soon as the movers shipped the furnishings. Knox had donated most of his furniture, but his mother had some family antiques she wanted to bring. They were starting a new chapter in their lives, and he wanted to forget anything that reminded him of Lola. Her parents lived in the neighborhood, not that they ever spoke to him or even Penny.

They blamed him. Maybe it was his fault that Lola got pregnant, but he'd accepted that responsibility. Their daughter was the one who didn't. Her father blamed him for, as he put it, *not keeping her in line.* With a father like that, no wonder Lola had escaped. Knox had called her father's thinking backward, and any family relationship they might have had plummeted from there. He realized they were never meant to be together, although Lola called it first.

"Kiss Penny goodnight for me," Knox said. "Call me if there is anything you need. And before you get on the flight."

"It's not as if we haven't done this before," Wanda said. "When your father was on active duty, we moved a lot. Maybe you don't remember that."

"I remember." Knox smiled. They had the same conversation over and over, but he didn't mind. He'd missed them. "Hey, Dad. There's a garden next door, and it sure needs your touch." His father had grown up on a farm and could grow anything. He loved working the land.

"I thought the house you're buying had a garden."

"A small one, but the other one is on an entire lot. The

other owner needs some help with it. She's willing to trade fruit for labor."

"Is that the woman who hoodwinked you out of that other house?"

"She outbid me, that was all. Paid cash for it, too. You know how sellers are. But we'll find another for you."

Doug looked thoughtful. "If you think she'd want me to help."

"I do. Her name is Junie. You'll like her."

His mother leaned in. "Is there anything we need to know about her?"

He knew what she was getting at. "Relax, we're just friends." Or were they? "Hey, I've got to go. I need to help on a job site."

"This late in the day?" His father beamed. "You're a hard worker, son."

The job site he was referring to wasn't exactly related to his work, but it was close enough. "I love you both, and I'll see you soon. Are you sure you don't need me to fly back to help with Penny?"

Wanda shook her head. "We're old pros at this. You stay there and work. And Penny is no trouble at all. Goodnight, honey." She signed off, and the screen went blank.

Knox knew Penny could be a handful, but his mother doted on her granddaughter. They would probably be fine without him. Knox had planned the move in detail, managing it as he would one of his construction projects.

He always took care to plan for every problem he could imagine. And he knew what could happen more than most project managers.

Knox had worked his way through high school and college on construction sites in New Jersey and New York, where the pay was good and the work was hard, especially in the freezing winter months. It had paid off, and he had graduated without owing anything. He'd met Lola after graduation at a neighborhood bar. They were young, but his parents had married even younger.

That part of his life was over. Crown Island represented a new beginning for all of them.

Knox leaned back in his chair and laced his fingers behind him, thinking about Junie and wondering how she would get along with Penny and his parents. He hadn't had much luck with women once they found out he had a child. That didn't seem to bother Junie yet.

Crown Island was a small town, and he didn't want to make any mistakes. Still, there was something different about her.

Since they'd talked at the fireworks, he hadn't been able to get Junie out of his mind. When he returned, he had stopped by the gift shop a couple of times, and she told him she'd gotten the keys for her new house. Today, he'd overheard Junie telling Faye that she was cleaning the house after work.

He decided to take a chance.

After checking the time, he punched a number on the house phone for the restaurant. "Hello, it's Knox MacKenzie, and I'd like to order take-out." He gave his order. By now, he'd practically memorized the menu. "Would you include extra napkins and utensils for two?"

Knox pushed back from his desk. He changed out of his trousers and bright Hawaiian work shirt into a T-shirt and jeans he had thrown into his suitcase. After combing his hair and splashing on some cologne, he left his room and took the stairs.

He preferred taking the beach route to the cafe instead of walking through the hotel. The air was fresh, and the ocean was calming. As far as he was concerned, this was the good life.

As he walked along the path, he nodded and spoke to others who worked at the hotel. Sailor, who was locking up the bike rentals for the day, and Faye, who ran a boutique across from Junie's gift shop. At the cafe that opened onto the beach, Knox signed for the food. He carried the bags to his rental car and got in.

A sudden thought occurred to him. What if she wasn't alone? He hadn't asked if she was dating anyone.

Knox blew out a breath. This was either brilliant or the stupidest idea he'd ever had. But he had dinner for two sitting beside him. He might as well risk it.

When he arrived at Junie's new house, she was outside, pulling weeds from a planter by the porch. He got out of the car.

She looked up in amazement. "What are you doing here?"

"Surprise supper." Knox hoisted a bag, which held two small pizzas and salads. He didn't know what she liked, but he hadn't met many people who didn't like pizza. "Are you here alone?"

To his relief, she nodded.

"You're an angel," she said, straightening with a small grimace. "This is harder than it looks, and I'm famished."

He couldn't take his eyes off her. Junie looked good in jeans and a T-shirt with her long sun-streaked hair piled onto her head. Different from how she looked at the hotel with her beachy cotton dresses, but still irresistible. More than that, she radiated happiness. Just seeing her lifted his spirits.

Tearing his gaze from her, he glanced at the wooden railing on the front porch, which needed to be secured. "After we eat, I don't mind helping you. That railing could give way if someone leaned against it. I'm not too bad with a hammer."

"You could do that?"

Knox laughed at the surprise on her face. "I worked my way through school on construction sites."

"So that's how you got your start," she said, taking off her gloves. "I was wondering."

"I'll tell you all about it over dinner."

She nodded. "But I don't have any place to sit. No furniture yet."

"How about here on the steps?" He brushed them off and spread out some napkins.

"Looks good to me," she said, brightening. "I'll wash up."

By the time she returned, Knox had laid out the pizzas, salads, and water bottles. "Your table awaits," he said, taking her hand. "Would you care for wine?"

"Would I ever," Junie replied, drawing a hand across her forehead.

"You deserve a break." After settling on the front steps, Knox brought out a bottle with two glasses from an insulated beach pouch he'd bought in a boutique at the Majestic.

Knox handed her a glass and held up his. "To new beginnings."

"My thoughts exactly," Junie said, touching his glass. "This is the first toast in my new house."

"We'll have to do the same in mine." Knox took a sip, admiring how the sun reflected in her eyes, which were a deeper shade of green than his.

"I'd like that, neighbor." She took a slice of pizza. "What kind of work did you do on construction sites?"

Knox picked up a slice. "How much do you want to know?"

"Everything." She blushed a little and added, "I mean, whatever you want to share. Besides this amazing pizza."

"That's all from Chef Gianna." Knox felt comfortable with Junie, and she let him talk. Unlike Lola, who had incessantly chatted about heavy metal music he didn't understand or care about.

As they ate, Knox told her about his first jobs, how they had moved around when his father was in the military, and how his mother had worked hard to help him overcome an early speech impediment. He didn't know why he had shared that, other than Junie was so easy to talk to. But most of all, he talked about Penny.

"I hope to meet her soon," Junie said, looking truly interested.

"Oh, you will." Knox shook his head, thinking fondly of his little girl. "She'll be running all over the yard in whatever costumes my mother makes for her."

"I used to do that, too," Junie said. "Capes were my favorite. I wanted to be a superhero. Or a librarian. Or a superhero librarian."

He chuckled. "I have to say, kids are a lot of fun. I apologize in advance if she bangs on your door or has a screaming meltdown that you can hear all the way over here."

"I can imagine," Junie said, laughing with him. "My

sister and I used to have such screaming fights. I don't know how my mother survived it all."

"And your father?"

"They're recently divorced," Junie said quickly. "We don't talk about him much. He lives in Seattle and just remarried."

Knox quickly changed the subject. "I met your mother when Ryan invited me for dinner. And I've seen the historical society building she's working on. She seems smart and talented."

"Thank you," Junie said. "We're pretty proud of Mom."

The smile returned to her face, and Knox relaxed. "I'd love to hear your story, too. Whenever you want to talk about," he added. "Or we can do some work."

Junie turned to look at the rickety railing and the plants that still had weeds in them. "All that will still be there tomorrow, I suppose."

"I can come by again and bring some tools."

A smile touched Junie's face, and she held up her empty glass. "We might as well watch the first sunset here."

Her easy smile lit his soul. This had been a brilliant idea, he decided. And tomorrow, he'd have to visit the hardware store at lunch.

17

"*H*elp has arrived," Maileah sang out as she stepped through the door of Junie's new house. She carried a box of cleaning supplies, rubber gloves, and rags.

"Where are you, sis?" She wrinkled her nose against the odor.

Junie had warned her about that, so she'd brought painter's masks, baking soda, and white vinegar. She wasn't sure what all that would do, but Nana told her what to buy and gave her money for it.

"In the kitchen," came Junie's muffled reply.

Maileah really needed a job. She was still at a loss as to what she could do. But for now, she could clean, much as she hated that. She wanted to support Junie, but she also had a plan.

"Why don't you hire someone to do all this?" Maileah said as she walked in to find Junie's rear end poking out of a lower cabinet. "You can afford it. And you've been at this for days. I would think you'd want to do something else on your day off."

Her sister had closed escrow on the house last week, and they'd thrown a party at Ella's house since this one wasn't even habitable. Since then, Junie had been a whirl-wind of relentless energy, scraping paint, yanking weeds, and cleaning endlessly—all while still working at the hotel. Maileah understood how excited Junie was, but her sister had to sleep, too. She didn't even come home for dinner.

Maileah shoved her box onto the counter and banged on the cabinet door. "Come out of there and talk to me."

Junie wriggled out of the small space, sat back on her sneakered heels, and removed her mask. Her T-shirt and jeans were filthy. She gasped for air but still smiled. "I sort of like cleaning. I feel like I'm getting to know the house."

"And all of its aches and pains," Maileah added, eyeing a cabinet door that hung lopsided.

Junie followed her gaze. "I can fix that."

"But can you fix that tragic color?"

"That calls for paint and lots of it." Junie brushed a cobweb from her hair. "Jo offered to gather people for a painting party."

"You realize there are people in this town who need work," Maileah said. "Don't be stingy, Junie. You're not a pro, and you can't do everything at once. Another day, and you'll be begging me to make rescue calls."

Junie swatted at the remaining cobwebs. "You have a point. Help me out today, and if we don't finish, I'll make the call. I want to line all the shelves and wash all the light fixtures. We'll need a ladder for that."

"And a man who can climb it."

Junie snorted at that. "I'm sure I can manage. I'm living

alone, so I must know how to do this stuff. But first, I want to get the kitchen up and running. I'm starving without one. But I need to clean the floor before the refrigerator arrives." She looked down with dismay. "Think I should replace it or just paint it for now?"

"About all that," Maileah said, sensing an opening. "I have an idea."

Just then, a deep voice rang out. "Hey Junie, I brought lunch. Time for a break."

"That sounds a little personal for DoorDash." Maileah poked her head around the door. "Oh, my gosh. Jamie from *Outlander* is marching through your house. What's going on?"

"Relax, that's only Knox," Junie said. "The guy who is buying the house on the corner. And he's overseeing construction at the Majestic."

"Where'd they find a specimen like him? I want to shop there, too."

"He used to work for Ryan on the East Coast. Now shush. And how's my hair?"

"A little Halloweenish. Just like when we were kids." Maileah reached over to pluck out the remaining cobwebs. "You really need to rethink this cleaning plan."

Knox strode into the kitchen carrying a bag that said, *Bon Appétit from The Majestic Hotel*. "Chef Gianna made a couple of paninis and salads for us." He stopped when she saw Maileah.

"This is my sister," Junie said, introducing them. "I was just telling Maileah about your job at the hotel."

"Wait a minute," Maileah said, frowning. "You two work together?"

Junie and Knox looked at each other, seemingly nonplussed.

"What's wrong with that?" Junie asked.

Maileah was appalled that Junie didn't know, but her sister had never worked for a large company. "Where I used to work, there was a corporate policy against fraternizing. Does Ryan know?"

Knox grinned. "That I'm bringing a fellow employee lunch?"

As Junie realized what her sister was referring to, her face flushed. "It's not what you think, Maileah."

Maileah covered her face with her hands. Now, she was the one feeling embarrassed. "I thought, well, I guess you know what I thought."

"We met again at the fireworks," Junie said. "Since we got off to a bad start—what with competing offers on this house—we decided to work at being good neighbors."

"If you say so." Maileah didn't recall seeing Junie at the fireworks, but then, she and Sailor had talked nearly all night.

Still, Maileah remembered how Junie had acted around Mark. She had that same silly smile now.

"And we're not exactly working together," Junie added. "The Majestic is a large place."

Knox put his bag on the counter. "If I'd known you were here, I would have brought something for you, too." He pulled out a wrapped sandwich. "But here, take mine. I'll grab another one back at the hotel."

"Or you can share mine," Junie said to him. "I'm not that hungry."

Hadn't Junie been on the verge of starvation two

minutes ago? Standing behind Knox, Maileah widened her eyes at her sister, but Junie only ignored her.

While Junie washed her hands, Maileah turned to Knox. "When do you plan to move into the other house?"

"As soon as it closes," he replied. "Should be another couple of weeks. I flew back to New Jersey to start the packing process."

"Are you going to live there alone?"

"Maileah," Junie said in a warning voice.

"It's okay." Knox grinned. "My daughter lives with me. So will my parents until we find a house in the neighborhood for them."

Maileah flicked another look at Junie. "Are you divorced?"

"I am now." He brought out two drinks and set them on the counter.

Knox's reply was curt, but that wasn't enough for Maileah. Especially given the expression on her sister's face. "So, what happened?"

Junie looked exasperated. "Come on, Maileah, leave him alone."

"Can't a big sister ask a few questions?"

Knox chuckled this time. "I don't mind. We married too quickly, and my wife wasn't ready to be a mother."

"Is she now?" Maileah asked.

"As a matter of fact, she travels with a rock band," Knox said. "She never visited Penny, and she relinquished her parental rights."

"That's cold," Maileah said. That comment earned her another sharp glance from Junie. "Well, it is."

"I agree." Knox shook his head. "If not for my parents, Penny's life would be awfully lonely. That's why they're moving with us. That and the sunny skies and mild weather."

They chatted for a few more minutes about things like weatherstripping and voltages that went right over Maileah's head. She wasn't ready for all that, but watching Junie, she had an urge to be on her own again, too.

"Wish I could stay to help," Knox said. "But I need to get back to the other construction job. Enjoy your lunch. See you later."

"Sure thing," Junie said.

He hadn't taken a thing to eat, Maileah noticed. She waited until he was gone. "Are you really seeing him later?"

"He understands construction, so he's been a huge help." Junie took a bite of the panini. "Wow, it's delicious today. Have the other one."

"How often does he bring you food?"

Junie shrugged. "Oh, I don't know."

Maileah laughed. "This explains why you've been working through dinner. We've hardly seen you. And you're certainly not starving."

"This house is a lot of work, and Knox has been so helpful. What's wrong with that?"

"Nothing. Do Mom and Ryan know you're dating?"

Junie threw up a hand. "That's not what I would call this. We're friends. Besides, how would you know? You're the one who's spending all your time with Sailor. I've seen you at the Majestic, mooning around the bike rentals. You don't even bother to see me, so I know what's going on, Mayfair."

That hit a tender spot in Maileah's heart. Sailor was such a good listener, and he made her feel special. But that was all. "Look, I'm sorry if I stole your date that night. I didn't mean to. We just talked, and you never came."

"Really, I don't mind at all," Junie said.

"Then you are interested in Knox."

Junie grinned. "I'd rather hear about you and Sailor."

"Sailor travels too much." Maileah shrugged as though it didn't matter to her, even though she would miss him. "I can't compete with all the teens and twenty-somethings idolizing him. He's flying out to a surfing competition in Hawaii, so you're stuck with me for a few days."

Her sister stared at her for a moment, chewing thought-fully, until Maileah finally pulled out the other sandwich. "Fine, I'll eat it." She took a bite. "So, what about Knox?"

"He's an interesting guy," Junie said. "But I don't know his family. I'm not getting involved with a guy unless I know everything I'm dealing with."

"No more mad, headlong rushes into love? How boring." Maileah took another bite. "Hey, this panini is pretty good."

"Thank Knox for that."

Maileah thought about this developing situation with her sister. It could be tricky, and she didn't want to see Junie hurt. "You shouldn't date someone who lives next door to you, especially when you're buying a house. If you break up, someone has to move."

Junie sighed. "There's a vacant lot between us. And we're still not dating."

"If you say so."

Narrowing her eyes, Junie asked, "What's up with you today?"

"Nothing. I just thought you might be lonely over here

by yourself. I could help you around here. Maybe even stay for a while. Living alone can be creepy at times."

Junie didn't answer right away, so Maileah tried a different approach. "We could have fun fixing up and decorating this old place just the way you want it."

"Deb and Mom have been helping me pick out things. But you can help, too."

Maileah appreciated that. "When I start working, I could pay rent."

"I don't need you to do that," Junie said, shaking her head. "The house is paid for."

"Then I could cover half the utilities, taxes, and maid service." Maileah gave her best big sister smile. "I love Mom and Nana, but they need their space, too. Just until I get on my feet again. I can cover for you in the gift shop, too."

"You have to be an employee and know how to sell."

"I worked in marketing, remember?"

Junie looked at her as if sizing her up. "Think you could handle blog posts, a mailing list, and social media?"

"Like a pro." Maileah gave her another broad smile. "It won't be for long. I know I should get out and meet people again. I didn't even know where Cuppa Jo's was."

"I'll think about it," Junie said, eyeing her.

Maileah figured she was at least halfway there with her sister. She finished the lunch Knox had brought and pulled on a pair of gloves. "Ready to work now. Tell me where you want me to start."

While she respected Junie's drive, Maileah was also willing to earn her way. If she lived here, Junie would force her to go out. Maileah loved their mother and grandmother, but they were so concerned they'd let her stay in her room every day if that's what she wanted.

Seeing Junie make such strides in her life inspired Maileah. Or maybe it kicked her competitiveness into high gear. Either way, this is what she needed.

18

"Here are some drop cloths to protect the hardwood floors," Junie said, handing them out to Knox, Blue, and Sailor. There were a couple of other new neighbors Jo had rallied as well.

Soon, her helpers were unfurling the cloths like sails and securing them over the old hardwood floors, which Junie planned to refinish as well. She and Knox had already removed the baseboards and would replace them afterward.

Junie had asked Faye to cover for her at the gift shop today so she could get the interior painting done before the furniture she'd chosen with Deb arrived.

"I brought the rest of the supplies," Knox said. He gestured to bags of painter's tape, brushes, rollers, spackle, caulk, and other tools.

"Thank you again," Junie said, grateful for his help. "I've painted before, but it was fairly basic."

"It's my pleasure to help, Junie."

Knox had been wonderful, referring different tradespeople through his connections at the hotel. He'd also been coming over every evening to do odd jobs. The railing on the front patio was now secure, as were the steps leading to the front door. The hinges on the cabinets were all working, and he promised to replace the runners on the drawers.

Junie was amazed at his work. He had also repaired or arranged to have things fixed she didn't even know needed attention, like the electrical and plumbing.

Knox passed out rolls of blue painter's tape. "Okay, team. Let's start prepping the walls. I'll show you some tricks of the trade." Everyone gathered around to watch how he filled imperfections in the walls.

Maileah turned to Junie. "What would you do without him?"

"I could have managed," Junie replied, feeling confident. "But it would have taken a lot longer."

Faye had been right about people coming out to help for pizza and beer. Jo had promised to arrive with food after the lunch run at the diner.

As Junie walked through the rooms to note any final details, she thought about how grateful she was for the friendships she had made here on Crown Island. Many people had come together to help her turn this old house into a home. One day, she would return the favor.

And she was especially grateful to Knox.

Pausing, she snapped a few photos with her phone to compare the before-and-after looks. She wanted to look back on all this.

Now ready to begin, she rejoined the group.

"Let's get this party started," Maileah said, waving a hand. "I brought the music." As she set up her playlist and arranged the speakers, everyone cheered.

Soon, upbeat music and the screech of tape rolls filled the air. The party was officially underway.

Once Knox was satisfied with the work people were doing, the group dispersed among the rooms. Blue and a friend from the neighborhood set to work on the primary bedroom while Maileah and Sailor claimed another one. Others began to tape off the bathrooms and kitchen.

Knox stayed with Junie in the living room. After they had prepped the room, he opened a paint can and poured a creamy light taupe shade she'd chosen into a tray. The smell of fresh paint filled the room, masking the old musty odor.

"This will look nice," Knox said. "I like the colors you selected."

"Thanks. I wanted to create a calm, restful ambiance." Junie had decided on soft, airy colors for the interior. "Wait until you see what I'm going to do with the outside."

"I know the island goes in for wild colors," he said. "What do you have planned?"

Junie spread her hands as if painting a picture. "It's going to bloom in shades of lemon yellow and peach, with those colors echoed in daffodils, sunflowers, and hibiscus." She had helped her grandmother enough to know what would grow here.

"Sounds happy," he said.

"For the garden, my mother and I found some antique wrought iron benches, as well as trellises and arches," she added. "I'm thinking of training yellow roses and passion fruit vines over those. Things grow quickly in this climate."

"Be careful there," he said, sweeping her hair back to keep the ends from dragging into the paint. "Want me to tie your hair back for you?"

Junie smiled at his thoughtfulness. "I'll tuck it up." She

twisted her hair into a knot and secured it with a pencil she plucked from his pocket.

"Pretty smart," he said, winking at her. "You've done that before."

"Once or twice," she said, smiling. Knox was so easy to be with, and she was growing accustomed to having him around. Still, Maileah's warning stuck in her mind.

Junie was excited to see how the interior paint would turn out. She planned to hire professionals for the exterior, as other repairs were also needed. She could hardly wait to see the house come together.

"I can roll on paint while you do the fine brushwork around the windows and doors," Knox said. "Is that okay with you?"

"Sure," Junie replied, picking up a brush. "As long as we can switch off so you can reach the higher parts. I'm pretty good with a roller, too."

"You're on," Knox said, grinning. "What a team."

Junie dipped her brush into a smaller container he prepared for her and began to apply paint around the window frames. Knox worked beside her, rolling paint onto the walls.

Junie was enjoying herself. "This is a lot more fun when you turn it into a party."

"That all depends on who's at the party," he said, chuckling. "I'm glad you're on my team."

"Thank you again," she said softly, touching his shoulder. "For this, for bringing food and christening the house with wine. For everything you've done."

Once again, Knox swept tendrils of hair from her face. "I just enjoy being with you, Junie."

"Hey, you two," Maileah called out, breaking the mood as she strode through the room. "Back to work."

"Mind your own business." Junie flung a little paint at her sister, who screamed with laughter and ran away.

As they worked, Junie enjoyed watching Knox. His hair had grown a little longer, and she liked the look on him. He was incredibly handsome, though he seemed mostly unaware of it.

Knox caught her gaze and smiled. "You're doing a great job." He nodded toward the wall she was working on.

He pulled out a step ladder for her so she could reach higher. "I'll get the top for you."

"This is going to look great," Junie said.

"Mind if I show off what we've done to Penny and my folks? They called this morning to say the movers came early. They changed their flights to arrive tomorrow. I'd really like for you to meet them."

"I'm looking forward to it as well," Junie said. A patter of excitement coursed through her, and she hoped they would all get along. "I'd love for them to come by. I might even have a few pieces of furniture to show off, too."

She liked eclectic design, so she had bought an antique pine table for the kitchen, and vintage bookshelves for the living room.

While they worked, they talked about their houses and plans. Junie could feel the chemistry between them growing. Occasionally, they brushed against each other as they reached for the tape or a brush.

Junie sensed a certain magnetism radiating from him, and she wondered if he felt that way, too. She also thought about his family and how their arrival might change things between them.

Although she couldn't deny her growing attraction to him, she was aware they might remain just friends. That would be okay, she decided, although that thought was edged with regret for what she thought could be.

Later, shortly after the noon rush at the diner was over, Jo arrived as promised. She carried a stack of pizzas Junie had bought. "Who's hungry?" she called out.

"Famished," Blue said. He rushed to clean his brush.

Junie smiled at the two of them. Jo and Blue really belonged together. Putting them together at the fireworks could have gone either way, so she was relieved when Jo told her they were dating again.

Soon, the entire group gathered on the front porch to eat, and Junie and Knox joined them.

After eating, Junie walked through the rooms, admiring everyone's work. Knox followed, also approving of what had been done.

"Paint completely transformed this place," Junie said, inspecting the newly painted walls. "It's amazing."

"It's getting there," he said. "There's still a fair amount to do, especially outside."

She took a step toward him. "Don't feel like you have to spend time here after your family arrives."

Knox tapped her nose. "I think we'll figure it out."

Junie wasn't sure what he meant. Was he referring to the house repairs or their budding relationship? But people began filtering in, so she let that question go.

The group returned to work. They were re-energized and ready to take on the rest of the job. As Junie continued painting, she and Knox chatted and made jokes. She noticed he was watching her a lot. A fluttery feeling filled her chest, though she tried to ignore it.

After all, he was just being friendly, right? Maybe this was all in her imagination.

As the night wore on, and the last of the painting was finished, people dispersed. Maileah and Sailor were the last to leave. Even her sister had done an amazing amount of work.

Soon, Junie found herself alone with Knox in the kitchen. He stepped closer, his eyes more intense than she'd ever noticed.

"Junie, I have a confession," he began, running a hand slowly along her shoulder. "We haven't known each other long, but I look forward to seeing you every day. I hope you're feeling the same way."

As he sent shivers through her, Junie rested her hand on his chest and closed the space between them. "I am. But are we ready for this?"

He didn't answer right away. Slowly, he said, "When my family arrives, if we don't have a chance to talk like we have been, I want you to know I'm not ignoring you." He rested his forehead against hers. "I love spending time with you, and I don't want this to stop."

"Neither do I," she said, encircling him with her arms. He felt so strong and warm in her embrace, and his heart was beating as wildly as hers.

"We'll be surrounded by family. But I think we can still manage," he added, sounding husky.

Junie had wondered if she might ever fall in love again. While it was still too soon to tell, a familiar, quiet knowing filled her heart. She had stepped onto a new path, and she would follow it to see where it might lead.

Yet, this new connection was as tenuous as a thread. Junie was realistic enough to know that it might snap with the busy responsibilities of family. Until she knew for sure, she couldn't risk the next step.

19

Knox watched the cherry-red ferry approach the dock. He had planned to pick them up at the airport, but his father preferred to rent a car at the airport and bring it across on the ferry. The family cars were being shipped as well.

Squinting against the sun, he saw his parents and Penny at the rail. His daughter's fair, reddish-blond hair was a copper beacon against the bright blue sky.

As soon as the ferry docked, Penny was first off. She raced toward him.

Knox knelt on one knee, holding his arms wide and bracing himself for impact. This was a game they played.

"Daddy!" Penny flung herself into his arms, nearly knocking him over with her enthusiasm.

"Hey, sweetie, I missed you so much. Give me the biggest hug you have."

Penny giggled, tightening her little arms around his neck. "I missed you, too, Daddy."

Wanda followed closely. Knox had inherited his dark

auburn hair from his mother. Now in her mid-fifties, she was still youthful and energetic. He thought she would get along well with Junie's mother, April. He greeted her with a hug.

"Where did Dad go?"

"To drive the car off the ferry. He'll be here in a moment." Wanda put a finger to her chin. "Now, let me take a good look at you. Something seems different."

"Aw, Mom." He hugged her again. "I'm really enjoying Crown Island, especially now that you're all here." They were his family, and he was so grateful for how they helped look after Penny.

His father drove the car off the ferry, parked, and got out. Doug MacKenzie was a barrel-chested man who still had an officer's posture. His cane tapped on the pavement, steadying his gait. Still, he had a bear hug for his son, too. "You're looking good, Knox."

"Thanks, Dad. You, too. I'm so glad you've come."

"This is so exciting," his mother said. "Penny has been thrilled the entire way."

Penny tugged Knox's shirttail, and he scooped her up. "I was good, too, Daddy. Right, Grammy?"

That was Penny's name for his mother. She called his father Pops.

"That's right, she was," Wanda replied.

"Follow me to the Majestic Hotel first," Knox said. "We'll stay there a few days while we get the house situated."

"I want to see my new room," Penny said, hopping from one foot to the other.

"I'll take us there next," Knox promised. "I ordered a

new bed for you, along with mermaid sheets. Those should arrive soon."

Knox had picked up the keys this morning and arranged a new furniture delivery for tomorrow. The rest of their belongings would take a few days longer to arrive by truck.

When they arrived at the Majestic, his mother was impressed with the elegance and beauty of the old hotel, while his father wanted to know all about Knox's new job and responsibilities. Penny darted around the lobby, exploring everything with wide-eyed glee.

Ryan strode toward them with Whitley beside him. "Mr. and Mrs. MacKenzie, it's good to see you again."

"Mom, Dad, you remember Ryan Kingston." Knox's parents had met Ryan in New York at the hotel where Knox had worked with him.

"Please, it's Wanda and Doug to you," Doug said, shaking hands.

Knox introduced Whitley, who was wearing a kiwi-green jacket. "Whitley is the general manager and heart of the hotel."

Whitley greeted them warmly. "Welcome to the Majestic Hotel. We have a nice suite of rooms for you."

"Anything but room 418," Knox said, grinning. Ryan had already warned him about the strange occurrences in that one. That was the last thing his mother and daughter needed.

They chatted while the front desk clerk confirmed their rooms. Knox had arranged a larger suite with adjoining bedrooms for her and his parents.

Once they had freshened up in their suite, they all piled into the car, eager to see the new house.

When they arrived, his parents exclaimed and made their way to the front door while he unbuckled Penny from her car seat. "Did you remember to bring Tubbles and Monksey?"

Penny turned her sweet face up to him. "They rode in my rolling bag so they wouldn't get lost. Grammy left them on my bed."

"We'll make a special place for them your new room."

He brought Penny out of the car and hugged her. He'd do anything in the world for his daughter, and it made him feel good to show her the house he'd bought for them.

"This is your new home, kiddo."

Penny screamed with excitement and raced to the front door. Knox followed behind. When he reached the front door, he slid the key into the lock. The door swung open.

"Why, isn't this lovely," his mother said, stepping inside the spacious living room. "And flowers, too."

Knox saw his real estate agent's card by the bouquet. "Kellie is a real peach, Mom."

"Is she?" Wanda asked, a note of interest in her voice.

Knox laughed at her intimation. "And she's your age."

"Your mother is already matchmaking," her father said, chuckling.

"Where's my room?" Penny was racing around the room, trying all the doors.

"Nope, that one's the closet," Knox said. "And the powder room." He grabbed her and flipped her onto his shoulders. "This way. Remember to duck." He bent his knees as he walked through the doorway.

"My, this is nice," his mother was saying as she walked through the rooms.

"The boy has done well," his father added.

"Here you go," Knox said, setting Penny down in her new room. "We'll fill this built-in bookshelf with all your books, and you have your very own bathroom."

Knox felt good about this house. He showed his parents their suite, which they liked. They moved on to the fully renovated kitchen and the outdoor barbecue, which his father loved.

Doug turned to the vacant lot next door. "Good grief, what in heaven's name is that eyesore?"

"That would be the garden I told you about."

Doug shook his head. "Better be an awful lot of fruit on those trees to make it worth my while."

Wanda smoothed a hand over his shoulder. "Oh, honey. You'll love working your magic."

"We're having a crew come in to clear it out so we can see what we have to work with." As soon as Knox spoke, he realized his mistake.

His mother picked up on it. "Who is *we*?"

"That would be Junie, the woman who bought the home on the other side that I told you about."

Wanda peered past the tangled garden and frowned. "Oh, my word. It's a little unfortunate looking."

"We had, I mean, Junie just hosted a painting party, so the inside looks nice. Nothing like this house, but it's good enough for now. The exterior is next."

"I suppose we should meet her," Wanda said.

Knox saw Junie's car. "Looks like she's there now."

He clasped Penny's hand. "Now, stay with me. There could be dragons living in that overgrown mess."

"Okay," she said in a small voice, shrinking into him.

He grinned. "Not really, but there are bugs."

They walked to Junie's house and knocked on the door.

That felt odd because he was used to walking in. Junie usually kept the door open for ventilation while she worked inside. Though he couldn't just walk in once she moved in.

She opened the door. "Well, hello there," Junie said, kneeling to greet his daughter. "You must be Penny."

Suddenly, the outgoing little girl turned shy. "Hi," she said in a tiny voice, gazing at Junie with wide eyes.

Knox introduced his parents. Junie was gracious, but he sensed she was a little nervous.

"Would you like to see inside?" Junie asked. "We just finished painting."

They stepped inside. The scent of fresh paint still lingered in the air.

"We heard about the painting party," Wanda said.

As his mother looked around, she chatted easily with Junie, asking her all sorts of questions about what she planned to do to the house, how long she'd lived on Crown Island, and what she did for work.

"Hey, Mom, go easy on her," Knox said. "You'll wear out the neighbors."

"I just like to know who is living nearby," Wanda said. "Especially when they're such attractive young women." She turned back to Junie. "Are you married, dear? Any children?"

"Mom, that's enough." Knox shook his head and turned to Junie. "You don't have to answer that."

"I don't mind," Junie said, smiling. "I don't have any children, and I'm widowed."

A hush fell over the group. Penny piped up, "What's that mean?"

"Oh, dear," Wanda said. "I'm so terribly sorry. How long has it been?"

"More than two years now." Junie darted a look toward Knox.

Wanda took this in thoughtfully. "Are you dating yet?"

"Not exactly," Junie replied, her face turning pink.

Knox cut off the questions. "Mom, really. You'll have plenty of time to get to know Junie later. Let's go. I'm sure Dad is hungry."

"We ate on the way," his father began.

Penny tugged on his shirt. "Daddy, what does widowed mean?"

By now, Knox felt torn, and Junie was smothering a laugh. Flustered, he picked up Penny, who was still asking questions. "All together now, everyone. Let's leave Junie in peace."

"Very nice to meet you, Junie, dear," Wanda said, lingering while Knox strode to the door. "You'll come over for coffee once we're settled. Are you sure you're not dating yet? A pretty young woman like you should—"

"Wanda, you heard your son." Doug took his wife's arm and winked at his son.

Turning back to Junie, Knox mouthed, *I'm so sorry.*

"Nice meeting you all," Junie said, before clamping a hand over her mouth to hide her laughter.

As he shut the door behind them, Knox turned to his family. "Well, now. That went well. Anyone else we should intrude upon while we're here?"

"But she's so attractive," his mother said loudly. "Have you noticed?"

"Maybe just a little. Come on, Junie might need her front porch." Knox hurried down the steps and angled toward the car. "Who wants to see the beach?"

Penny clapped her hands. "I do, Daddy."

Knox managed to corral everyone into the car. After he shut the car door, he tilted his head back and ran a hand over his head.

Was he delusional for thinking that this would work with Junie? His life was chaotic at best. She'd met him on his own and had no idea what she was getting into. He was sure nothing could have prepared Junie for his mother's inquisition.

Frankly, he hadn't seen that coming. At least, not quite to that degree. He thought they'd have ten or fifteen minutes of good behavior.

He could plan an entire hotel renovation, but he never knew what sort of chaos his family would serve up. Still, he loved them fiercely, so he had to laugh.

Well, that's that, he thought, glancing longingly at Junie's house. He wondered if she would ever want to talk to him again.

He could only wait and see.

20

*J*unie plopped down onto the convertible sofa bed mother had bought. "You won't have to sleep on this much longer. My furniture is being delivered soon."

"It's going to be quiet around here without you and Maileah," April said. "We'll miss you."

Junie looked up, surprised. This was news to her. "Excuse me?"

Maileah rushed around the corner. "I might have told Mom and Nana that I was going to be staying at your house. Not exactly moving in. Just until you're comfortable being by yourself."

Junie sat up. "We talked about this, Mayday." Her sister was high maintenance, and Junie hadn't decided. She had been looking forward to having some privacy with Knox whenever he could manage.

Yet, her sister's face held such a hopeful expression. Junie sucked in a breath, recalling how Maileah had once supported her. When Junie's world was at its bleakest, her sister had hounded her, urging her to get up and get out. Maileah had an unusual way of showing her love, but it was there. Besides, their mother and grandmother probably needed a break.

Junie patted the cushion beside her. Maileah needed her now, so she would be there for her. "Come here, you. Tell me which room you want."

Maileah leapt toward her. "I won't be in the way at all. I'll give you and Knox all the privacy you want."

April looked surprised. "You're dating Knox?"

Maileah shrank away from her. "Oops. Sorry, Junie."

"I'm not sure what we're doing, Mom."

Maileah shook her head. "I told her it wasn't a good idea since they work together at the hotel."

Now Junie was even more appalled. "Maybelle, don't you have something you need to do?"

Her sister snapped her fingers. "You're right. I should pack." She flounced off the sofa and disappeared down the hallway.

Junie drew her hands over her face. "I was going to tell you, but she beat me to it. Do you think this is a bad idea?"

"Why, no," April said. "I was just surprised, knowing how you felt. Do you know much about him?"

"He's been helping me with the house and bringing me dinner. I even met his parents."

Maileah poked her head around the corner again. "Gosh, that sounds serious."

"Out." Junie threw a pillow at her. "Do you want to move in with me or not?"

Maileah ducked and ran.

"You'd think we were still kids," Junie said, pressing a hand to her forehead. "I don't know how this is going to work out. She might drive me bonkers, but she was there for me."

"Yes, she was," her mother said, nodding. "Families can be challenging. What are Knox's parents like?"

Junie wasn't sure how to describe them. "They seem nice, but they're a little chaotic. In a fun way, though. I wasn't expecting that." She spread her hands. "I like his mother, but she is already trying to play matchmaker."

"With you?" A smile played on April's face.

"Knox hasn't told them anything. And honestly, Mom, there isn't much to tell."

"But you've been spending a lot of time together, according to your sister."

"We've been getting to know each other." Junie considered this. "We didn't want to take our relationship to the next level until I'd met his family. But oh, Mom, his daughter is so precious. Penny is her name, and she's six years old. She has the sweetest little angel face and the prettiest coppery blond hair. And it's clear that she loves her daddy."

"Do you know what happened to her mother?"

Junie nodded. "Her mother left when Penny was an infant. If that little sweetheart were mine, I would never let her go."

Junie's words hung in the air until April cleared her throat. "Living so close, you'll have ample opportunity to get to know him and his family. But you haven't told me how he makes you feel."

That was a good question, Junie realized. She had never tried to put it into words. "I'm not sure where to begin. He's nothing like Mark, but I wouldn't expect him to be." Junie closed her eyes, recalling the moments they'd spent together. To her surprise, she hadn't been thinking about Mark as much as she used to.

A twinge of guilt tweaked her heart, but she thought Mark would understand. He had loved her, and she felt he wouldn't want her to be alone anymore.

Her mother put her hand over hers. "Knox is probably just as special in his own way."

Junie nodded, her eyelids fluttering as she struggled to find the words. "When he looks at me, the world falls away," she whispered, pressing a hand to her heart. "Sometimes, I can hardly breathe when he's around. Yet, I feel so calm, too. As if I am meant to be right there with him. It's as if we belong." Junie opened her eyes and sighed. "I never thought I would find this feeling again."

April reached for a tissue and handed it to Junie. "That's beautiful," she said, taking another one for herself.

It was then that Junie realized tears had trickled onto her cheeks. She wiped them away and looked down at the dampened tissue, evidence of her feelings. "I hardly know what to think, Mom."

"Then don't." April took her hand. "Ryan is very fond of Knox, and everyone speaks highly of him. Although I had no idea about you two, I like him very much. You have good instincts, so simply follow your heart again." She swept her arms around Junie. "I'm very happy for you."

Junie rested in her mother's embrace. "Mom, there's something else I need to tell you."

"What, darling?"

"Last night, I had such an incredibly vivid dream." Junie blinked against tears that flowed again, but she went on. "Mark was holding me, just like you are. The next thing I knew, he was walking away into the brightest light I've ever seen. He turned and told me I would always be loved. Then he disappeared. I felt oddly light. As if I could float."

Just then, her grandmother appeared in the doorway. Ella smiled. "I would say that Mark released you. What a dear man he was."

"You heard all that?" Junie asked, blinking as if coming out of a trance.

Ella nodded. "I didn't want to interrupt. But I had a similar dream about my dear Augustus."

Even now, Junie felt like she was recalling an actual event. "It seemed so real."

"Maybe it was," Ella replied, stroking Junie's hair. "Who's to say?"

21

*S*eated at the little study desk in the bedroom that had been her mother's, Junie tapped the print button on her laptop computer. While her work printed, she stretched. She had worked hard on this presentation, in part to keep her mind off Knox.

Since he had visited last week to introduce his family, he'd gone silent on her. She had seen him only in passing at the hotel. No calls, no texts, no knocks on the door. Every time she caught a glimpse of him at work, it hurt. However, if she'd acted on her feelings, it could have been much worse. Sadly, she had been wrong about him, yet she learned she still had the capacity to love.

But she had more important things to do now.

The name of her new business shone on the screen: Crown Island Princess.

This was the written plan and financial projection for the business she wanted to start. She had an appointment with Ryan today at the Majestic Hotel. Sharing this with him was risky because he might review it and decide the hotel could create this without her.

She had been working on branding for the Crown Island Princess. The theme was tropical luxury living with a vintage edge. Artisan jewelry, island fashions, accessories, and beach housewares.

When she created her new assortment for the Majestic Hotel gift shop, she had to stay within a certain budget. But for a business of her own, she could source beautiful items and negotiate on her own. Having already run a successful online business, she was confident she could do this but was nervous about presenting it to Ryan. Yet, being affiliated with the Majestic would give her business a boost and be good for the hotel.

She had to make him understand the value of the venture for the Majestic. However, she hadn't talked to Ryan much about business. Whitley had hired her, though Ryan was the decision-maker on this project.

Maileah tapped on her door. "These were on the printer. Are they yours?"

"Thanks," Junie said, holding out her hand for them.

Instead of giving her the papers, her sister lingered by the door reading them. "This looks interesting. You're planning to sell handcrafted jewelry and fashions?"

"Most items are from Crown Island artisans," Junie replied.

Maileah flipped through the presentation. "And a luxury line of Majestic Hotel goods?"

Junie rose from the small desk and plucked the printed pages from her sister's hands. "That's confidential."

"Your resume looks good. And the projected financials."

Junie arched an eyebrow at her. "You know how to read the numbers?"

"I had budget responsibility at my last job."

"I didn't know that."

"There's a lot you don't know about me," Maileah said, joining her. "I have plenty of skills but not many places to use them here."

Junie recalled a prior conversation they'd had. "You told me you could write blogs and manage newsletter campaigns."

"And a lot more in marketing." Maileah sat cross-legged on the narrow twin bed. "The Crown Island Princess. Love the name, and it sounds like a good plan. Are you quitting your job at the gift shop?"

"That's what I'm pitching to Ryan this afternoon." Junie organized the printed pages as she spoke. "I'm trying to lease that space because I see an opportunity for a much larger online business—for me and the Majestic."

Maileah nodded thoughtfully. "That would be cool if he goes for it."

Junie glanced at her sister and smiled. "Did you know you're partly responsible? What you said about me being stuck in a hotel gift shop got me thinking."

"I didn't mean that." Maileah grinned. "Well, maybe I did. I try to look out for my little sister."

Junie smiled at the memory. "I hope Ryan goes for this idea. That's why I've included the hotel's profit projections and cost savings. The management team already turned me down once, but I didn't have any of this prepared. My mistake."

"Listen to you," Maileah said, lifting her brow. "I'm impressed. You're pretty talented, too."

Junie appreciated that. "I did more than buying shoes and casual clothes for our online business. I had to develop a wide range of skills. Mark ran the technology side of the business while I juggled everything else."

"Say, I have an idea for you." Maileah clicked her fingernails in thought. "I used to go to events in Los Angeles that were set up for celebrities. The large fashion and tech companies would give away their latest merchandise, hoping to get photos of celebrities using their gadgets or wearing their clothes."

Junie was aware of this practice, but she had never participated. "I couldn't afford to do that. Besides, it's not my style." Still, it was interesting that her sister was thinking marketing angles.

Maileah twirled a strand of hair. "Maybe not, but I know some of the stylists. I've seen a few placements rocket a new product or brand to the top. I think I could call in some favors. Especially if a free weekend at the Majestic was involved."

Junie's lips parted in surprise. "That's a very interesting idea. Hey, you're not so bad."

"I'm not bratty all the time. Just when we're having fun." Maileah looked a little sheepish. "But seriously, I can help you. It would be fun. And I'd feel a lot better about living at your place if I'm doing something to help."

"Maybe we can put the craft room to better use," Junie said. "You'll need a place to work."

Maileah sat up straight and saluted her. "Princess Number Two, reporting for work. Let's do this, even if Ryan doesn't go for it."

"It would be better if he did." Junie stood and tucked the pages into a folder. "Wish me luck."

Maileah leaned forward. "Have you seen Knox at work?"

Junie hesitated. He hadn't been by the gift shop, but she hated to admit to Maileah that she'd been right. "We're just friends now."

Maileah folded her arms. "He ghosted you after his family arrived, right?"

"It's not that. Knox is busy, and so am I."

That much was true. Junie had been meeting people at the house before going to work. She and Maileah had been painting cabinets every evening.

Junie was tired but happily so. Her life was mostly looking bright. She closed her folder and picked up her purse. "Don't forget, furniture and appliance deliveries are tomorrow, so you'd better be up early. I need you."

AFTER ARRIVING AT THE MAJESTIC, Junie waved to Stafford, the retired elevator operator who still entertained guests at his table in the cafe. She loved the vintage ambiance of the Majestic, and she knew many others would, too.

Yet, she was a little nervous. Even though Ryan was from a modest background here on Crown Island, he had traveled and worked around the world. Some of his investors were billionaires, and Knox had worked for him on a high-profile project in New York.

While Junie's plan was important to her, it was a small matter to Ryan. She almost hated to bother him, especially since he had already declined her project. But Junie was determined.

She opened the door to the executive offices. *Round two,* she thought to herself.

"Hi, Junie," the receptionist said, looking up when she entered the office suite. "Mr. Ryan is expecting you."

She walked into his office. Ryan was standing by a window, looking out to sea.

"Thanks for seeing me," Junie said. While she saw him on Beach View Lane, he was usually with her mother, so they rarely talked about business.

After greeting her, Ryan leaned on the edge of his large desk and regarded her with interest. "I wondered why you wanted to talk again after Whitley shared our position."

"Honestly, I didn't convey all the advantages to the Majestic. You should have the full picture." She brought out her folder and opened it. "This time, I've prepared a business plan for the venture, along with projections, to demonstrate. I call it the Crown Island Princess. And Gift Shop," she added quickly.

Ryan smiled. "You want to lease the space, but I need to show a profit to investors. Do these numbers do that?"

"And a lot more." She quickly outlined the project she had in mind. "It's luxury island style meets the Majestic."

"Interesting. May I have a look?"

Junie shared her documents with him, and he scrutinized the numbers with a practiced eye. She was impressed by how quickly he grasped the idea and the potential.

"I'll take this to the board as a different project, leading with your concept and showing the advantage of having your company partner with us. I wasn't fully aware of your accomplishments with your former company, so including your resume was a good idea." He rubbed his jaw. "Leasing the space can be seen as a bonus for us."

"I'll still carry toothbrushes," Junie said. "Luxury style, of course."

Ryan chuckled. "Before Knox checks out your space, I'll ask him to see how we could carve out a small part for toiletries."

Junie was surprised, but the mention of Knox's name derailed her thoughts. And Ryan noticed.

He arched an eyebrow. "You have met Knox, haven't you?"

"You don't know?" Junie wondered how much her mother had shared with him.

"Know what?"

A little embarrassed, Junie shifted. "We were bidding against each other on a house on Sunshine Avenue."

Ryan grinned. "And who won?"

"I did," she replied.

He laughed and tapped the folder she'd brought. "I'll make sure this goes to the board for final approval right away. I think we've found a diamond on the beach. In you and this project." He smiled. "You're a lot like your mother."

"Yes, I am." Junie bumped knuckles with him and left his office.

As she passed Whitley's office, she was surprised to see Knox with him. And as she left the executive offices, she heard Ryan call out to him. "Got another job for you, Knox."

She hurried back to the gift shop, relieved that the meeting had gone as well as it could. Her mind was buzzing with ideas. Between this new concept and her beach cottage, she really didn't have time for Knox MacKenzie anyway.

22

"This pine table goes in the kitchen," Junie said to the delivery truck driver. She put her hands on her hips, surveying the barely contained chaos on Sunshine Avenue.

One of the movers put the table down and began to push it across the hardwood floor.

"Watch the floors," Junie cried. "Put some cardboard under those legs or pick it up. I just had the floors sanded and refinished."

Over the past week, Junie had enjoyed shopping for furnishings and organizing the house. Moving was strenuous work, but she was thrilled to have a place to call home.

That balanced her disappointment over Knox, who had virtually disappeared except for rare sightings at the hotel. And just as she had opened her heart to him. In fact, he still hadn't visited the gift shop as Ryan had requested. She hoped to hear good news about the Crown Island Princess project soon.

However, Knox's parents seemed to be everywhere she

turned. Doug had been nosing around the garden she had cleared, so she ordered plants and put him to work. He was thrilled. Wanda had befriended her mother and grand-mother, while adorable little Penny followed her from room to room.

She still had no explanation of what had happened with Knox that last day, but she was glad she hadn't gone any further in their relationship. Clearly, he had only been inter-ested in having company until his family arrived.

In the parlance of Maileah's dating terminology, she suspected she had been ghosted. Her sister was right. Dating a neighbor wasn't such a good idea.

Pushing aside her wounded heart and pride, she went outside to look for her sister.

Maileah stood on the street by another van, directing men carrying boxes marked *office supplies*. "Put those in the room with the Crown Island Princess sign on the door." She turned to Junie. "Aren't you glad I'm here?"

"You're earning your keep, that's for sure," Junie said, slinging her arm around her sister's shoulder. "Sisters forev-er." While their relationship had been volatile, she was feeling better about it after all they'd been through with their parents.

The cartons were from her home with Mark that she had tucked away. When her mother moved from the house in Seattle, she had brought them with her, and they'd sat in her grandmother's attic. Junie couldn't recall what had been packed. She had been in such a haze that her mother did most of it for her.

Junie expected to find photos of her and Mark that she'd had on her desk. She had decided to dedicate space to him on her wall of family photos in the hallway. Finally, she was feeling at peace with what had happened.

This was a new era now, and Junie was pleased that everything was coming together in her sweet little cottage. Beds were being delivered today. She and Maileah would soon spend their first night in the house.

Her mother was in the kitchen now, cutting lining paper to fit the drawers and shelves. Junie had turned over the kitchen organization to April, who was much better at that and enjoyed it. Deb had stopped by as well, and the two of them were talking and laughing.

Junie had put just enough work into the house to make it comfortable. She and Maileah had finished painting the cabinets in the kitchen and bathrooms. A sleek new refrigerator and stove would be delivered later today, and an electrician would install new ceiling fans. The delivery of a washer and dryer was also scheduled.

She appreciated everything Knox had done and wished he could see how the house looked. He had been so helpful in guiding her.

Junie was amazed at how well the hardwood floors had come out. They were even better than new, in her opinion. The honeyed shade brought warmth to the house, and the minor imperfections were a testament to all who had lived in and cared for this home before her.

In her bedroom, Junie had placed a multicolored handwoven silk rug that her mother and Deb helped her select at a local antique shop. In the rest of the rooms, she arranged sisal and soft rugs she could wash. Beach life could be messy, and she didn't want to worry about a little sand tracked into the house.

Even though the cottage wasn't perfect, Junie loved her

new home. She intended to embrace her life ahead regardless of what it might hold.

At the blue corner house on Sunshine Avenue, a similar level of activity was going on. Junie watched with interest, although it wasn't any of her business. Still, that didn't stop Wanda from visiting, especially when she learned Deb was an interior designer.

A tap on the pavement sounded behind her. "You'll never guess what we've uncovered in the garden," a voice bellowed.

Junie turned. "What's that, Doug?"

"A thriving herb section. Rosemary bushes as big as boulders, and enough ginger and garlic to open a restaurant. Oregano is growing wild, too." He began talking about preparing the garden for planting right away. "We'll be just in time to plant the summer crops. Tomatoes, peppers, cucumbers."

"I won't have time to look after all that," Junie said.

Doug waved off her comment. "Don't worry about that. I'm an old farmer at heart. So is Wanda. We like puttering in the garden."

"So do I, when I can," Junie said. "I'll happily provide whatever plantings you think we might need. I love summer salads."

She'd already acquiesced to the idea of a shared garden. It would be too much for her to tend to—or eat. And her new neighbors seemed excited to have the space. She understood why Knox had been keen to buy her property with the extra lot.

Just then, Wanda called out, "Doug, where are you?"

"Talking to Junie. Come join us."

A delivery van parked in front of their home pulled

away from the curb. Wanda hurried toward them with
Penny skipping beside her. When the little girl saw Junie,
she raced toward her.

"Come see my room," Penny said, jumping with excitement. "Grammy said you can."

Wanda caught up with them, her seashell earrings
bouncing as she walked. "We've had such fun decorating
her beautiful room. It's so precious. Just like her."

"Why, I'd love to." Junie waved to her sister. "Can you
take care of things? I'm going next door for a few minutes."

Maileah nodded with a grin, and Junie sighed.
Everyone from her sister to her mother and Wanda were
holding out hope for her and Knox, but it wasn't to be.

"Let's go," Junie said, taking Penny's hand. The six-
year-old was so excited, Junie had to trot to keep up.

She stepped inside the MacKenzie home and was pleasantly surprised. Compared to her house, this one was
modern and spacious. It still retained its original character
but had been fully, beautifully renovated. No wonder Knox
fell in love with this home.

"This way," Penny said, rushing toward her room.

Junie glanced back, but Wanda hadn't followed her. She
was outside talking to Maileah now.

Penny raced into her room and hurtled onto the bed,
bouncing gleefully on a mound of pillows in the shape of
mermaids, shells, and starfish. "I love it, love it, love it. So
do Tubbles and Monksey." She hugged a well-loved stuffed
bear and monkey.

Junie laughed. "Wow, so do I. It's like we're under the
sea."

The little girl's bedroom was magical. From the
mermaid-themed comforter to the ocean-inspired lamps,

pictures, rug, and wall decals, it was just as Junie would have decorated it.

Someday, she thought, she might have a chance with a family of her own. Was that still meant to be for her?

"Look at my giant clamshell," Penny screamed, falling face-first into an enormous, squishy silver pillow on the rug. She dissolved into gales of laughter and reached for Junie, pulling her off balance.

"Whoops!" Junie crashed onto the huge stuffed pillow beside Penny, laughing along with her.

Penny started tickling her, and if there was one thing Junie couldn't control about herself, it was that. She screamed. "Oh, no! You're a tickle monster!"

"What's going on in here?" Knox appeared in the doorway, frowning at them.

"Oh, my gosh," Junie said, completely mortified. "What are you doing here?"

He folded his muscular arms. "That's my line."

Junie tried to catch her breath. "Your mom...and Penny...wanted me to see her room. I didn't know you were here." She rolled off the pillow and tried to stand, but Penny roared like a tiger and jumped on her, flattening her on the squishy giant clamshell.

As she was flailing around, Knox stepped in. He scooped up his daughter with one hand and held the other out to Junie.

"I can get up by myself," Junie said, ignoring his hand. She rolled over, but her legs got tangled in a plush mermaid throw. Desperate to get away from Knox, she gave it a good kick.

"Ow," Knox cried, looking surprised. "You kicked me."

"I didn't mean to," Junie said. "This blanket thing..."

Knox clenched his jaw. "If you'd calm down, and let me help you—"

"Play with us, Daddy," Penny said, wriggling from his grasp. Then, she hooked his belt loop and yanked him down.

"Penny, don't!" Knox yelled, stumbling onto the over-sized, squishy cushion on top of Junie. His daughter jumped onto his back, screaming with laughter.

"Ooof," Junie cried, the wind knocked out of her. Her nose was smashed into the plushy clamshell.

Penny grabbed pillows from the bed, happily pummeling them with starfish and mermaids.

Just then, Wanda appeared in the doorway. "What on earth is going on in here?"

"I did it, Grammy. I did it!" Penny scrambled off and hopped around them.

"Did what?" Wanda asked.

Penny pointed to her father and Junie. "Got those two together, like you said we needed to."

A guilty expression washed over Wanda's face. "Well, I didn't mean quite like this. Come on, sweetheart, let's get a snack for you." She took Penny's hand and swept her from the room, closing the door behind her with a quick smile.

23

"*C*an't breathe under here," Junie said. Her throat was scratchy from all the screaming and laughing. And Knox was partly sprawled on top of her. She tried to ignore how tempting he felt.

He rolled off the plush clamshell pillow and landed on the rug with a thud. "I am so sorry about Penny. Are you okay?"

"Besides being mortally embarrassed?" She raised a limp hand. "Maybe I do need help. I seem to be trapped."

Knox rolled onto his side to face her but made no move to help. "I know what that feels like."

Lifting her head, she narrowed her eyes at him. "If you mean trapped, as in living next to me, I want to remind you that I was here first. You'll have to live with that. And I'm not leaving." She let out a huff. *Maileah was right.*

"Neither am I," Knox said, staring at her with eyes she could fall into forever.

"Fine. That's settled." She struggled to get up.

"Not so fast," Knox said, blocking her with a seashell pillow. "We need to establish some rules."

Clearly, he was upset that she was here. In his position, she probably would have been, too. "I didn't know you were home."

"Do you make a habit of traipsing over when I'm not?"

"No, I was invited." She brushed her hair from her face. "Penny wanted me to see her room. Where's your car?"

"In the garage."

"Well, if I had known you were here, I wouldn't have come." She tugged at the octopus-like blanket that seemed to grow tighter the more she struggled against it.

"And why is that?"

She glared at him. "Because you've ghosted me."

"What?" He furrowed his brow and looked confused.

"Ghosted. Ignoring me. Not giving me a reason why you broke off whatever we had. It clearly didn't mean anything to you."

"Oh, no," he said, shaking a finger. "You were the one who did that."

"Me? How do you figure that?"

"After you met my parents, I didn't hear a word from you."

She stared at him, slowly realizing he was serious.

"It's not the first time this has happened," he added, sounding weary. "Not many women want a man with a full-time child and nosy parents who live with him. But this is my life. And now you know."

Junie kicked her legs again. "I don't believe this."

Knox untangled the blanket. "There. You're free to go. Can we at least be civil to each other?"

Could she bear that? *This is it*, she thought, sensing his

vulnerability. In a panic, she realized they might never have this chance again.

"Absolutely not." Junie grabbed him by the shoulders and did what she'd been dying to do. She threaded her fingers through his thick auburn hair and planted a kiss on his full lips—lips that turned out to be just as sensual as she'd imagined.

"What are you doing?" he asked, sounding breathless.

"Leaving." She pushed him away. "Sorry, I just had to do that. So you know what you're missing." She rocked to her feet.

"Oh, no, you don't." In an instant, he pulled her down, and his lips were on hers with an urgency that took her breath away.

Yet, just as every cell in her body was succumbing to him, Knox pulled away. She dropped back onto the plushy clamshell, panting for breath. Every fiber in her body ached for more.

"That was so *you* know what you're missing," he growled.

Junie laughed. "You're not getting away with that." Shoving him again, she wrapped her arms around his muscular shoulders, melting into the deliciousness of him again.

This time, neither of them pushed the other away.

A few minutes later, they emerged from Penny's bedroom, their hair mussed and their faces flushed with emotion. But they had put Penny's room back as they had found it.

Outside, Wanda was pushing Penny on the tree swing in the front yard.

When Penny saw them, she asked loudly, "Were they

kissing like you said, Grammy?"

"Maybe," Wanda replied, winking.

So MUCH IN Junie's life had changed in the past few weeks, from her address to her relationship status. Far from being alone in her new cottage as she had feared, friends and family now surrounded her.

This morning, her house rang with laughter and chatter. She and Knox had decided to have a joint housewarming party so they could meet their neighbors and welcome friends. Jo had circulated their invitation on Sunshine Avenue and around the neighborhood.

It wasn't even noon, but the sun was bright, and people were pouring in with their families to introduce themselves. This party would be an all-day affair.

Jo sniffed the air. "You might want to check those muffins."

"Thanks for reminding me," Junie said, grabbing a pair of bright yellow oven mitts.

Her mother and Deb were seated at the antique pine table in the kitchen with Wanda, sharing opinions on the best child-friendly beaches on Crown Island.

Through the kitchen window, Junie noticed Doug and Penny in the garden, checking on the newly planted vegetables. Two other children about Penny's ago skipped beside them. And farther away, Junie saw Knox standing on the porch of his home, greeting people.

"The muffins look ready." Junie pulled a tray from her new stove. "Hot lemon poppyseed muffins if anyone is hungry. And Maileah is making another pot of coffee."

"You can put those right here," Deb said. "They'll go

with this new lemon-print tablecloth. Where did you find it?"

"From a local artisan." Junie had been scouting for suppliers for her new endeavor and discovered many artists and craftspeople. Crown Island had a fascinating tradition in the arts.

While the women compared notes about other items they'd found at different shops in the village, Junie turned to her mother. "Do you think Ryan might come today?"

"I doubt it," April replied. "He's been busy at the hotel all week. Some of his investors are in town, and he needed to meet with them. Haven't you heard from him?"

Junie shook her head. "The last time we spoke, he sounded confident about my plan. This delay isn't a good sign."

April smoothed a hand over Junie's arm. "If your idea isn't approved, you could find another retail space."

"Maileah is working from here, and I could, too," Junie said. "But it would be advantageous to work out a deal with the hotel because of the built-in foot traffic. I'd rather not have to find and transform another space. This house has been enough work." And it still wasn't finished.

April patted her shoulder. "Try to be patient. I'll let you know when I hear from Ryan. Now relax and enjoy the day. I see a lot of new faces here."

That was true. Laughter trickled from the living room where neighbors had gathered.

"There are more people than I expected," Junie said. "Do we have enough ice for the drinks?"

"Not really, but I could send one of the guys out for more," Maileah replied. "We have plenty of food, though. It's an eclectic feast."

"It's always like this," Jo said, bustling into the kitchen. "Everyone loves to eat. That's what keeps me in business."

"Did you bring your famous sweet potato fries?" Junie asked.

"I'll bring a plate in here before they disappear," Jo said. "Want some grilled brussels sprouts sprinkled with parmesan cheese? They're new on the menu."

"Bring them on," Maileah said, and everyone joined in.

This morning, the aroma of food filled the air. Neighbors had brought enchiladas and quesadillas, chips and guacamole, cheese wedges, and vegetable trays. With such a large crowd, everyone had pitched in for a potluck feast. Junie had set up folding tables in her dining room to accommodate them. She hadn't found the table she wanted yet, but she had plenty of time.

Having Maileah here was a huge help. Her sister was helping to unpack and organize, and she was there to oversee workers when Junie was at work.

"Hey, Junie," Faye said, appearing in the doorway. "Is there any ice for the lemonade?"

"In a minute," Junie replied. She had an idea. "I'll be right back. Maileah, would you send someone? It's going to be a warm day."

Her sister was feasting on the brussels sprouts Jo brought in. "One more and I'll go."

Junie piled a handful of sweet potato fries into a small bowl and hurried out the rear door. Outside, she couldn't help glancing back to admire her home. A splash of sunny yellow paint with white trim and peach accents had brought the house back to life. The color made her feel so happy.

She entered the garden that Doug had been overseeing under an arch. Waving at him and Penny, she walked across the winding stepstones they'd discovered under the growth they had cleared.

When Knox saw her, his face lit with a smile. He excused himself from the group he'd been talking to and met her halfway.

"Hello again," he said, greeting her with a soft kiss. "Can you believe how many people have turned up? And to think I was worried about Penny making friends."

"She's so curious and smart." Junie was becoming as enamored with the little girl as she was with her father. "She was planting seeds with us the other day."

"I'm glad you two get along so well," Knox said, watching Penny with love. "You don't know how much that means to me."

Junie placed her hand on his heart. "I think I do."

Knox plucked a crispy fry from the bowl. "Are these for me?"

"I need a bag of ice," Junie said. "Want to trade?"

Knox gestured toward the house. "I have extra bags in the deep freeze. Come with me."

Junie tucked her arm through his, and they made their way toward the screened-in porch off the rear of the kitchen.

Knox put down the bowl of fries and ran a hand along the latch of the wide, low-standing deep freezer. "Would you give me a hand here?"

"What do you need?"

Knox grinned. "This." Swiftly, he picked her up and deposited her on top of the unit so she was at eye-level with him. Cradling her face in his hands, he let his lips linger on hers, teasing her a little before giving her the sweetest kisses.

When he was finished, Junie smiled against his lips.

"Must have been good fries."

"Not as good as you." He touched his forehead on hers. "Do you realize how lucky we are to have found each other?"

She sank her head against his broad chest. "Every day."

They had been seeing each other as often as possible, usually after he tucked Penny into bed. Once, Junie helped Wanda prepare a fresh seafood catch, and they all ate together. Another evening, when Maileah was out, Knox arrived with a bottle of wine. They had sat on her front porch, talking about their dreams.

Just then, slow footsteps sounded on the pathway outside. Knox put his finger to his lips, and they waited to see who it was.

"Probably kids," she whispered.

But it wasn't. Whitley and Ella were strolling arm in arm. They were laughing and talking as if they were more than friends. He stopped and plucked a wildflower for her.

"I feel like we're spying on them," she whispered.

"That's because we are," Knox replied.

Suddenly, Junie stifled a sneeze, and Knox chuckled.

"Why, who's there?" Ella called out.

"It's us, Nana."

"Come in," Knox said, opening the door. "Junie needs some ice at her house."

Ella looked at Junie, amused. "It's probably right under you, dear."

Knox lifted Junie from the freezer. "Thanks. We've been looking for that."

They all laughed while Knox opened the lid and reached inside. He brought out two bags of ice. "This should last for a while."

"What are you two doing back here?" Junie asked.

"Just having a little stroll," Ella said. "We heard the house behind yours might come up for sale soon. And walking is good for our health."

"We always have a lot to talk about," Whitley added, looking into Ella's eyes.

Junie nudged Knox. "So do we." They could talk for hours, but she sure was enjoying his kisses now.

Ella turned to them. "You've both had profound life experiences at a young age, and you're more mature for it. Because of that, you probably have more in common than with many your age."

Whitley gazed at Ella with pride. "That's a wise observation."

Junie wondered if that was part of the attraction or why they connected so well. Looking at her sister, who had not been married, lost a spouse, or been a single parent, she could see the difference between her and Maileah.

Whitley glanced at the ice bags. "You don't want those to melt."

"Oh, right." Knox took Junie's hand.

Junie winked at Ella as she and Knox left them on the porch. Junie wondered if there might be more to her grand-mother's relationship than she would admit.

Music was playing now, and Junie guessed that Maileah had something to do with that. People were gathering in one area of the yard to dance. Penny waved and ran to join them. "Can we ride our scooters?"

"Under an adult's supervision and only in the drive-way," Knox said. "We left it on the screened-in porch. Whitley can help you if you need it. And make sure Pops is watching you."

"Thanks, Daddy." Penny took off again, with another child racing beside her.

His father waved to him, and Knox gave him a thumbs-up. "Looks like he's got this. Mom and Dad help me keep a close eye on Penny."

He turned to the house behind his. "Imagine that. Another house for sale. Wonder what it's like?"

"I see what you're thinking." Junie stood on her tiptoes to see it. "Looks nice. I promise not to bid on it."

"I should contact them before word gets around," Knox said. "That would be a great location for my parents. We should think ahead." He squeezed her hand.

Junie only smiled, wondering what he meant. For now, they were happy, and she was enjoying her new home. She would rather let their relationship unfold naturally than force it.

They continued toward Junie's house, where Knox deposited the ice in Junie's kitchen. "You can bring more of those hot fries anytime."

"I'll keep that in mind," she said, laughing.

Her mother was still sitting at the table with Deb. April looked up. "Oh, there you are. Ryan just saw the last of his investors off on the ferry. He is on his way here."

Knox knew how much this meant to Junie. "Do you want me to stay?"

"I don't want to bombard him with questions as soon as he arrives."

Knox agreed with that. "We should move the food and drinks outside. That way, everyone can be together."

"You have the larger yard," she said. "Let's gather there. People can spill into the garden, too."

They had uncovered several old seating areas on the lot

and erected umbrellas over second-hand tables they'd found.

"I'll have Maileah move the music," Junie said. "Neighbors can wander through the house. They're all curious about the work we've done. My house was the neighborhood eyesore for so long."

"Not anymore," Knox said. "Now, when I look out the kitchen window, this sunny house makes me smile." He hugged her. "Let's ramp up this party. We have a lot of new neighbors to meet. And I want them all to know you're taken."

"Ditto," she said, laughing.

"Oh, look, here's Ryan now," April said, rising to greet him.

Ryan walked into the kitchen. When he saw Junie, he broke into a broad grin. "Do I have news for you."

"Well, don't keep her waiting," April said.

Ryan ran a hand over his hair and chuckled. "You two are an awful lot alike."

"I think that's a good thing," Junie said, shifting from one foot to another. "Well?"

"Congratulations," Ryan said. "My entire team loves your Crown Island Princess concept. You'll have a letter of intent next week, and then we'll work out the details. You've just worked your way out of a job and into a partnership." He raised his hand for a high-five.

"That's fantastic," Junie cried, smacking his hand. Excitement bubbled up in her, and Knox hugged her.

"I knew you could do it," April said.

Just then, Maileah appeared in the doorway. "Maybe I heard wrong, but did you just get fired?"

"Sort of, and it's the best thing ever." Junie laughed

and put her arm around Maileah. "We have a lot of work ahead of us." Junie could hardly wait to flesh out her idea.

The party continued, and the music brought everyone outside. Neighbors strolling by stopped to visit and meet them.

When Maileah turned up the music, everyone started dancing. Junie danced with Penny and Knox; she could hardly remember when she'd had so much fun.

After a few hours, the party wound down. Maileah and others pitched in to clean up, and Junie appreciated that. Her sister's attitude was changing, and Junie was happy for her.

Knox returned, wrapping his arms around Junie. "Mom is bathing Penny, and she and Pops will tuck her into bed and read to her. I think they kicked me out on purpose. Want to catch the sunset on the beach?"

"I'd like that," she said. Sharing the sunset was a time-honored tradition on Crown Island, and she could think of no one she'd rather share it with.

Knox reached for her hand, and they started off toward the beach. It was only a couple of blocks away.

When they reached the beach, they slipped off their flip-flops and strolled barefoot along the water's edge. With a waning moon, the waves were gentler this evening. The balmy air and the light sea breeze felt good on her warm skin.

"It's been quite a day," Junie said, dangling her slides in one hand.

"It's been more than that," Knox added, putting his arm around her. "When I stepped off that ferry, I had no idea how my life was about to change."

As they walked, they watched the waves and chatted about the people they'd met at the party.

Knox smiled at her. "This is shaping up to be a good neighborhood. At first, I wasn't too sure about my new neighbor, but she's growing on me."

Junie gave him a playful swat. "I could say the same thing."

Soon, the sun hugged the horizon, and the day slipped away. Golden rays fanned into the sky, slowly deepening into dramatic streaks of fiery orange and dusky purple.

Junie rested her head on his shoulder. "It's a gorgeous sunset tonight."

"Just like the company," Knox replied, turning to her.

The sky illuminated his eyes, reflecting the colors of the heavens. But more than that, Junie saw deep emotion on his face. She sucked in a small breath. This new wave of feelings was real, and she could hardly believe the second chance life was serving up.

Knox was gazing at her with the same expression of awe.

She knew the chance of finding a soulmate twice in a lifetime was infinitesimally small. Yet somehow, the fates had conspired to do just that. What were the chances they would both land on this sunny island in the Pacific Ocean? She and Knox had won against all odds.

Beside her, Knox cleared his throat. "Junie, it's amazing that we found each other, and just when I'd decided not to date until Penny graduated—despite my mother's match-making efforts."

"Wanda never gave up hope," Junie said, smiling. "I still laugh when I think of that first day when I met her.

Honestly, I didn't know quite what to think, but I adore her now."

"I'm glad you do." Knox chuckled. "That nearly ended our relationship. Her efforts were counterproductive."

"So that was the real secret why you were still available," Junie said. "I'll have to thank her for keeping you off the market until we could meet. And you must admit, she staged our reunion in Penny's room very well."

"She's taking credit for that," he said, chuckling. "But she can't claim credit for how I feel about you." He touched his chest. "That comes from deep within my heart."

"I feel that way, too," Junie said softly. This was the moment; the moment that flowed so naturally yet changed everything.

Knox swept her into his arms. "I love you, Junie. More than I ever dreamed possible."

His heart was beating as rapidly as hers. "I wasn't sure I could love again," she said softly. "But you've shown me the way."

Knox drew his hand over her cheek. "My life is complicated, but I would love you to be part of it. Forever, if we're so fortunate. We still need to learn more about each other, but you're the one for me. Do you understand what I'm trying to say, darling?"

"I do, and I feel the same way." A proposal was too soon for them both, but the intent was there. She'd known real love once, and in his eyes, she recognized it again.

They came together in a kiss, sharing the depth of their feelings.

Junie smiled at him. "We both know what we want," she said, stroking his face. "Which is all the sunshine this life has to offer."

AUTHOR'S NOTES

BONUS! Thank you for reading *Sunshine Avenue*. Want to read a little more about Junie and Knox? I have an extra scene that didn't quite fit, and I thought you might enjoy it. Visit my website at www.JanMoran.com/SABonus. Enter your email address to receive your bonus scenes by email. (If you don't have access to a computer, ask a friend to print these for you.)

Can't wait to find out what happens next on Crown Island? Read Maileah's story in *Orange Blossom Way* and continue following the whole family. Maileah has several issues to overcome, but she is working on them. Will she be ready to make her dreams come true when the opportunity arises?

Keep up with my new releases on my website at JanMoran.com and don't forget to shop exclusive ebook and audiobook bundles, coffee mugs, and bookmarks ONLY on my bookshop at store.JanMoran.com.

Please join my VIP Reader's Club there to receive news about special deals and other goodies. Plus, find more fun and join other like-minded readers in my Facebook Reader's Group.

Want more beach fun? Check out my popular *Summer Beach* and *Coral Cottage* series and meet the boisterous, fun-loving Bay and Delavie families, who are always up to something.

Looking for sunshine and international travel? Meet a group of friends in the *Love California* series, beginning with *Flawless* and an exciting trip to Paris.

Finally, I invite you to read my standalone family sagas, including *Hepburn's Necklace* and *The Chocolatier*, 1950s novels set in gorgeous Italy.

Most of my books are available in ebook, paperback or hardcover, audiobook, and large print. And as always, I wish you happy reading!

LEMON POPPYSEED MUFFINS

When Junie bakes these lemon poppyseed muffins in *Sunshine Avenue*, I can just imagine the fresh, inviting aroma in the kitchen. Poppyseeds add a nutty flavor and slightly crunchy texture to these sweet, zesty muffins. These are sunny treats any time of year.

Bakers have a few tricks to create muffins with puffy tops. One is to increase the heat at the beginning, then lower it after a few minutes without opening the oven, as instructed in this recipe. The other is to chill the dough before using it. An hour or so will work but overnight is better. Even without that, these are yummy muffins. Yet another trick is to use special muffin tins that are more shallow and allow the puffy top to spread.

You may also use butter instead of oil (increase by 20% if you do, as oil has more fat than butter, so muffins might not be as moist). Reduce the sugar if you're watching your sugar intake. I often use a sugar substitute in baking, so feel free to experiment.

When you bite into these tasty muffins, I hope you feel like you're visiting Sunshine Avenue.

Yields: 12 large muffins

Ingredients:

2 1/2 cups (300g) fine cake flour, or all-purpose flour
2 tablespoons (15g) poppy seeds
2 teaspoons (10g) baking powder
1/2 teaspoon (3g) baking soda
1/2 teaspoon (3g) salt
1 cup (200g) granulated sugar
1/3 cup canola or vegetable oil (80ml)
2 large eggs
1/4 cup (60ml) fresh lemon juice (from about 2-3 lemons)
Zest of 2 lemons
1 cup (240ml) milk

Simple Syrup Lemon Glaze (optional)

1/3 cup (100 ml) granulated sugar
2-3 tablespoons (30-45ml) fresh lemon juice
2 tablespoons (15g) coarse sugar (to sprinkle)

Instructions:

1. Preheat the oven to 400°F (200°C). Line a muffin tin with 12 paper liners or lightly grease.

2. In a large bowl, mix flour, poppy seeds, baking powder, baking soda, salt. Set aside.

3. In a separate mixing bowl, mix oil (or softened butter) and granulated sugar until light and fluffy or about 2 minutes.

4. Add the eggs one at a time, mixing well after each one.

5. Stir in the lemon zest and fresh lemon juice. The mixture might look slightly curdled.

6. Gradually add the dry ingredients to the wet ingredients, alternating with the milk, beginning and ending with the dry ingredients. Mix until just combined; be careful not to overmix, as this can make the muffins tough.

7. Spoon the batter into the prepared muffin tin, filling each cup about 2/3 full. For higher-topped muffins, fill the tins more. Note: Chill batter 1 hour or overnight for added rise.

8. Bake in the preheated oven for 6-8 minutes. Reduce heat to 350 F (175 C) for 12-16 minutes, or until a toothpick inserted into the center of a muffin comes out clean or with just a few crumbs. Do not open the door when reducing heat.

9. While the muffins are baking, if desired, prepare the lemon glaze by whisking the sugar and lemon juice in a saucepan over a low flame until sugar is melted.

10. When muffins are done, remove from the oven and allow to cool in the muffin tin for about 5 minutes. Then, transfer them to a wire rack to cool completely. If left in the muffin tins, the bottoms may become soggy.

11. Once the muffins have cooled, brush or drizzle the lemon glaze over the top of each muffin. Garnish with a sprinkle of coarse sugar.

These lemon poppy seed muffins are refreshing for breakfast or as an afternoon snack with tea. May be stored in an airtight container for up to 3 days.

ABOUT THE AUTHOR

JAN MORAN is a *USA Today* and *Wall Street Journal* bestselling author of romantic women's fiction. A few of her favorite things include a fine cup of coffee, dark chocolate, fresh flowers, laughter, and music that touches her soul. She loves to travel, and her favorite places for inspiration are those rich with history and mystery and set against snowy mountains, palm-treed beaches, or sparkly city lights. Jan is originally from Austin, Texas, and a trace of a drawl still survives, although she has lived in Southern California near the beach for years.

Most of her books are available as audiobooks, and her historical fiction is translated into German, Italian, Polish, Dutch, Turkish, Russian, Bulgarian, Portuguese, and Lithuanian, and among other languages.

If you enjoyed this book, please consider leaving a brief review online for your fellow readers where you purchased this book or on Goodreads or Bookbub.

To read Jan's other historical and contemporary novels, visit JanMoran.com. Join her VIP Readers Club mailing list and Facebook Readers Group to learn of new releases, sales, and contests.

Made in the USA
Middletown, DE
17 October 2023

40967505R00137